BROKEN

Book 3 of the Daniel Briggs Novels

C. G. COOPER

"BROKEN"

GET A FREE COPY OF THE CORPS JUSTICE PREQUEL SHORT STORY, *GOD-SPEED*, JUST FOR SUBSCRIBING AT CG-COOPER.COM

DEDICATIONS

To my loyal group of Novels Live and Beta Team warriors,
thanks for your undying enthusiasm.

To our amazing troops serving all over the world, thank you
for your bravery and service.

And to the United States Marine Corps: Keep taking the
fight to the enemy.
Semper Fidelis

CHAPTER ONE

"I would just say there is one misperception of our veterans and that is they are somehow damaged goods. I don't buy it."
- General James "Mad Dog" Mattis, (USMC, Retired)

PIKE PLACE MARKET - SEATTLE, WASHINGTON

You become accustomed to the smell. Most people think fish markets smell like rotten fish. They don't, at least not the good ones. When I first arrived at Pike Place a couple months before, the first thing I noticed was the chill. It might have been the breeze coming off the Puget Sound, or the cold emanating from the iced down displays in the market, but that day I scarcely felt it.

I'd never been to Seattle before. When I got there, my first impression was how cold it felt, despite the fact it was June. Now it was August, and though the weather had changed, and the sun shone a bit brighter, I still laughed every time I left for work and a little nip tickled the back of my neck.

Instead of slinging fish like the guys up front, I was busy

keeping the deck clear of ice and debris with long strokes of a broom or squeegee. I didn't even smell the fish anymore. It had become part of my existence. I am sure I would notice it if I were to go away for a while and return.

So as I swept the floors for the umpteenth time, my mind drifted from memory to memory, but I vigilantly scanned the growing crowd. It was still early morning, but the locals and tourists had already packed the popular market.

Vendors called out to passersby. Parents called to their children, warning them not to get too far ahead or to not touch the neat rows of squid. I watched it all, finally content after months of travel. I'd arrived in Seattle by train, taking the long way across the US in what I thought might be my last trek.

Somewhere along the way, the passing vista dulled the cutting edge, calming the blaring memories to a dull roar. In the past, when I'd stepped off a train or bus in a new town, my first stop would've been the liquor store to pick up my good friend, Jack Daniels. But not this time.

The trip had soothed my thirst. I'm not sure when it happened, and I can't say I was surprised. Jack was a good friend, a brother whose sweet lullaby had coaxed me to sleep during the worst times of my past. But it looked like Jack and I might be done for good.

I smiled at the recollection while I swept up another in a long line of fish scales with my sure and thorough broom strokes.

"Hey, Briggs, get another pack of snapper, will ya?"

It was Angelo, a swarthy Italian who'd somehow ended up in Seattle. How? I had no idea, but he was a decent boss. I nodded my assent and went to the back of the market.

When I returned with the square bucket of fish dangling from one hand, I had to push through the crowd, excusing myself along the way. It was Saturday, after all, and it looked like visitors were gawking and buying at a rapid pace. The snapper was almost gone when I finally got to the front of the display. Thanks to Angelo's weekly special, the fish was selling briskly.

Angelo was, at the top of his lungs, serenading his guests with his traditional Italian tunes. I never had a clue what he was singing, but by the twinkle in his eyes, I wondered if the song was something lewd. But the people stopping to stare and clap didn't seem to care. They loved the show; they loved Angelo. Me, they barely noticed.

With the last fish stacked, I brushed the hair from my face using the back of my hand. It was getting longer now, unruly really. I'd never had long hair, and at times I contemplated getting it cut. But something else always came up, and Angelo kept me too busy give it much thought. He didn't really care and only occasionally gave me a hard time about the length.

As I made my way through the crowd again, I noticed a slight form walking by. She was old and walked with a hunch, like time had been unkind. She wore a long overcoat, and her eyes were always searching the crowd. She was a regular at Pike Place, like a lost dog looking for a home. She never said a word to the vendors, but picked out passing tourists or grocery-laden locals, pointing to the laminated picture hanging from her neck. It was a picture of a soldier, one of those official photos taken at boot camp or soon after arriving to your first unit. I'd only glimpsed the image, but the guy looked like a baby-faced newbie, just like the rest of us had then. I imagined there was probably a picture of me floating around from Parris Island, with me looking serious at a mere sixteen years old.

I didn't know who the kid in the picture was, but if I had to guess, it was probably her son. It was in the way she looked pleadingly at strangers as she pointed to the image. I'd asked

Angelo about the woman once, and he'd answered with a slow swing of his head and a sad closing of his eyes.

The old lady made her way further into the crowd. Just like that, she was out of sight and out of my mind. I resumed my tasks of keeping things clean and spent the rest of the day at Angelo's beck and call.

BY CLOSING TIME, the sun was far out to sea, the last embers smoldering over the horizon. I was cleaning out the old ice while Angelo and two of his fish handlers, Derek and Kurt, helped the owner in the back. I heard Angelo humming as I took my time making sure everything was wiped down and certain nothing was left on the display.

Out of habit, I always kept one eye on the street. I wasn't necessarily paranoid, but old habits die hard, right? I mean, when you spend the most formative years of your life around fellow Marines looking over your shoulder and through rifle scopes, how do you shake that habit? You don't.

But the beast inside of me was idle as I finished my nightly duties. I didn't have anywhere to be; my mere existence was now either working or sleeping. I would rather have worked all night than to drift off into fitful sleep, even if it wasn't as torturous as before.

So I cleaned up the market, keeping an eye and ear on the street, always wary and alert. As I scooped up the last bit of ice stubbornly clinging onto the bottom of the case, I heard shouting from up the hill. My ears perked up for a moment, but I recognized the sounds immediately. There were always teenagers coming and going when the crowds thinned. They liked to go down to the water and make noise. They cussed at each other, or hassled lingering strollers until they got bored or a cop showed up to usher them away.

I didn't know why they did it. Probably out of boredom,

but I really didn't care. It was none of my business. It was best to keep my head down.

I saw them out of the corner of my eye, ribbing and pushing each other until the smallest of the four gave the hardest shove. He was rewarded with a punch in the arm for that, but he didn't seem to mind. There was always one runt in any bunch, the kid who was either scrappy or just plain stubborn. From what I'd seen of this familiar bunch, this group was no different.

I pegged their ages to be somewhere between seventeen and twenty. They posed no threat to me, but I still kept one eye on them as I gave Angelo a thumbs-up, indicating my work was complete. As I picked up my trusty broom and wet dust pan, I heard the teenagers mocking someone on the street. They all laughed and the taunts stopped, only to be resumed when they apparently found a new target.

For them, it was harmless fun at another person's expense. It was entertaining for them, but it was not so much fun for the person on the receiving end. I wondered what might happen if one day the young men ran into the wrong mark.

Then I heard laughing again, and when I turned to see what caused the ruckus, I saw the lady in the overcoat. She was surrounded by the four boys. Even from that distance, I could sense her fear, her eyes wide with alarm as she tried to avoid making eye contact with the bullies.

"Who's the kid in picture, Grandma?" the largest of the four asked.

"I'll bet he's a faggot!" jeered the runt.

"Yeah, I'll bet she's advertising faggots," said another, a lanky teen with cheeks riddled with acne.

I tried not to watch.

It was none of my business.

But my body stiffened, and I stopped my retreat to the back of the shop.

"You got any money, Grandma?" asked the runt, poking the woman in the stomach with his finger. "I know you've got money."

The others laughed as the runt tried to pry the woman's coat open. She backed away, seemingly more concerned about protecting the picture than her body.

Angelo apparently heard the commotion because he came out and stood next to me. He wasn't a small man, probably a couple inches over six feet, and he was strong from years of hauling and flinging fish. I was surprised when he hesitated to help.

"Leave it alone, Briggs. They won't hurt her," he said, already retreating back to the market.

"I need to help her," I said, stepping away from the fish stand, my eyes taking in the rapidly deteriorating scene.

"Someone will call the cops, I'm sure," said Angelo behind me.

I barely heard his warning as I stepped off the curb, my eyes locked on the scuffle. My pace quickened as the runt pushed the woman to the ground, her head smacking loudly on the pavement.

They must have heard me coming because they all turned in unison.

"What the fuck do you want, fish boy?" inquired the tallest kid, who probably had four inches on my near six-foot frame. He had beady eyes set far apart, like some deep sea fish that rarely saw the light of day.

"Leave her alone," I insisted, not slowing down my pace.

The lanky kid stepped out first, unlucky for him.

My open palm whipped out like a snake, slamming him hard in the chest, knocking the wind out of his unfortunate lungs. He staggered backward. It took the other three a second to figure out what had just happened.

The big guy ran at me like an angry bull. I watched him

come, the inches between us closing. This time my foot snapped out straight, my heavy boot stopping the kid's momentum cold as his groin connected with my best shot. His eyes rolled back in his head as he toppled to the sidewalk.

I stood with my feet a shoulder width apart, the broom still in one hand. The runt and his last standing buddy glared at me, but now there was fear in their eyes. It was palpable, like the cold wafting off a block of dry ice.

"Take your friends and go," I warned. Dead calm descended upon them. It was laced with the absolute certainty they would be next should their decision-making skills flop like their idiot friends.

They didn't say a word. Somehow they dragged their co-conspirators away.

"I'll get that fucker later," I heard the runt say under his breath. I was already kneeling down to check on the old woman. Her prized picture was torn, but I was more worried that they'd inflicted permanent bodily damage. A moment later, she turned onto her side, her hands covering her face like she expected to be hit or kicked.

"It's okay," I said. "They're gone."

She didn't move for a few seconds. When her hands left her face, she immediately began searching for the crudely laminated picture. I could see it better now. It was a photo of a young soldier, his eyes brimming with pride and a touch of uncertainty concerning what might lay ahead. He looked like a thousand other soldiers I'd seen; no distinguishing features. Just another warm body in a camouflage uniform, trying to look tough for the camera.

"My picture. It's torn," said the woman. Staring down at the photograph, she stroked the young man's face like a mother might soothe a sleeping baby.

"Is there anyone I can call?" I asked.

She didn't seem to hear me, so I again inquired, "Ma'am, how can I help you?"

At that, her eyes darted back to mine. "Can you help me find my son? Can you help me find my poor boy?"

I didn't know what to say, and by this time there was a crowd gathering. Without a way out, I said the only thing that came to mind. "Of course, I'll help you find your son."

CHAPTER TWO

H er name was Rose, and Angelo suggested I take her home. She didn't complain. In fact, she didn't say a word and just started walking.

I followed her as she slowly picked up steam. She kept her head down, plodding the familiar path as if pulled by some unseen tether. No words were spoken, and I kept a respectful distance behind her.

I watched her as we walked, noticing that she took short, sure steps rather than using the shuffling gait of a homeless beggar. She seemed suddenly younger, like the outer shell was some sort of disguise. The "old me" might have been suspicious, thinking that maybe the old woman was drawing me into a trap.

But the "new me" pushed that thought aside, genuinely curious about the woman I'd seen so many times, but only now had the chance to truly observe.

Rose stopped abruptly and stuck her hand into one of her pockets. It returned holding a single key. She pivoted left and ascended a short flight of stairs to a barred door. There was a keypad to the right of it. She quickly entered her code, careful not to let me, or anyone with a wandering eye, see what she was typing.

The door buzzed and a moment later we were inside. The hallway was only slightly wider than just enough to accommodate one person, and the dimly lit passage smelled like a hundred old apartment complexes I'd been in before. It reeked of old paint, wet carpet and stale body odor. It made me cringe because this was no way for the poor woman to live. I wondered what I might find as she made her way to the end of the hall into a rickety stairwell that led up to the floors above.

Rose lived on the top floor, and when we entered her hallway, I noted the change. The smells from the first floor were gone. Instead, I noticed the tang of old bricks and home cooking rather than the rank stench of a poor man's tenement.

The door to her apartment was plain and chipped in a few places. There were scratch marks near the bottom lock where someone had tried to break in. Rose slipped another key out from her pocket to unlock the door strangely enough, the two locks on her door were not keyed to the same master.

We were greeted by a comforting warmth as the door opened. I guess I didn't know what to expect, but what greeted me was anything but what I'd imagined.

The apartment was one large room, literally a flat, with a bed in one corner and a kitchenette in another. There were books everywhere, neatly tucked in discrete alcoves, stacked in orderly piles on flat surfaces, and some dog-eared books perched on window ledges. Other than the books and knick-knacks, the place was as tidy as a Marine gunnery sergeant's office. It smelled of mint and bitter tea leaves. It was soothing in a way, like a visit to grandma's, or at least what I imagined a visit to grandma's to be like. I never knew my grandparents.

Rose let me in, still without a word, and then secured

each of the four security locks on the inside of the door. I waited as she went about her routine, her fingers nimble on the mechanisms. The place looked well lived-in. I wondered what she did for money, considering her daily pilgrimage to Pike Place Market and wherever else she wandered during the day in her quest to find her son.

"Can I get you some tea?" she asked, already making her way to the kitchenette.

"Yes, please."

She didn't acknowledge my presence as she set about the task of boiling water and muddling sprigs of mint in two over-sized coffee mugs.

I stood patiently, my eyes wandering around the room until they fell upon the corner opposite her bed. I wouldn't call it a shrine, but it was pretty close to it. There were so many pictures. Some were wallet-size photos and some as large as eight by ten. The photos were of her son in a little league baseball uniform and one in a cap and gown, but the overwhelming majority were of him in various Army uniforms. In one photo, he was in the desert (Iraq would be my guess). I remembered my old buddies taking the same pic, holding machine guns, smoking cigarettes, or just posing, looking tough in full-combat gear. We all did it, some more than others. Mostly, we took the pictures because we were bored, but some wanted to show off to their friends and family back home.

When he did smile, it was a proud smile, as if he belonged in the uniform. It made me wonder what had happened. Before I could ask, Rose said, "That's my boy. His name is Jonathan." She never looked up from whatever she was doing with the tea.

"Army?"

She nodded in affirmation.

"What did he do?"

Rose didn't answer but grabbed both mugs. She made her way across the flat and handed over a steaming cup.

"Thank you," I said, taking a tentative sip. I wasn't much for tea, but something in the combination of the mint and herbal drink made me smile. There was a hint of sweetness, maybe honey? "It's very good."

Rose nodded again and went to the corner dedicated to her son.

"He wanted to be some kind of Special Forces. I don't know what they're called," she said, holding the mug like its warmth was giving her the energy to speak. "He talked about it all the time in his letters, told me about the places he could tell me about, and how much he loved being with his friends. He was proud and I loved him for it."

There was a sadness there, like the punch line was about to come. But instead of continuing, Rose just stared at the pictures, like a weary loneliness had gripped her again.

"He looks like a good kid," I said, not knowing what else to say. It had been so long since I'd spoken to anyone that way. It wasn't really my thing, but watching her stand there, so reverent and sad, moved something inside me.

Finally, she turned and faced me. The sadness was gone, replaced by a new look, one of curiosity.

"Why did you help me?" she asked.

It caught me by surprise until I realized why she'd asked. It had happened before, and by the intensity with which she asked, I knew no one had lifted a finger those other times.

"I had to help," I said, once again at a loss for words.

"Thank you," Rose said.

We stood there for a long moment, neither saying a word.

"You remind me of Jonathan," she said, still curious, like she really did see something in me that reminded her of her son. I didn't know why she thought that; I had blonde hair and he had brown. While he was skinny, I was more on the lean side.

"How so?" I asked, taking a sip from my tea, savoring the subtle flavors that I still couldn't place. Maybe it was her special recipe.

"He was always helping others, my Jonathan." And then her eyes lost their luster again, like a fog had suddenly descended into the room. "He *was* that way."

I could see her mind was drifting again. I'd seen it before, traumatic injuries or events causing moments of lucidity followed by anger or just apathy, like what Rose was now exhibiting. I was no doctor but I could see the change.

"What happened to him?" I asked, figuring that the blunt question was what she was really waiting for.

If my bluntness surprised her, she didn't show it. Instead the clarity returned and she began her story.

"Jonathan enlisted at seventeen. He'd always wanted to serve, and some of his uncles were in the Army, so I guess he just thought that was the way to go. He was never an athlete, but he made it sound like boot camp wasn't so bad. I went to his graduation, and even though I didn't necessarily want him to serve, he looked so happy, so proud to be part of something good. That was just after 9/11.

"After that he reported to his unit, and he always called me when he wasn't training. We hadn't been close when he was a teenager, but something about the Army brought him back to me. I was so grateful. He visited me when he could, and one time I flew to see him. It was wonderful to see him in his element. He was taking classes, trying to get his degree, and he'd even met a girl. It should have surprised me when he called to say he was getting shipped out to Iraq, but it was all over the news and I'd expected it. For some reason I didn't think of the possibilities. I thought we'd go in there just like in Desert Storm and come right back out. Well, that didn't happen. During the first deployment he stayed for a full year. At first his letters were upbeat; some of these pictures came with them. But toward the end of his tour, I noticed his tone had changed. He was coming up on the end of his enlistment, and he had a choice to make. Part of him felt like he had to stay to be with his fellow soldiers, but I could sense the weariness in him, like so many things were taking a toll."

She stopped for a moment and looked at me.

"Have you been to war?"

I nodded.

"And you saw your friends die?"

I nodded again, willing my body not to tense. I hoped there wouldn't be any further questions about me. I didn't want to be rude, but there were some things I did not want to discuss.

She didn't press further and turned her attention back to the pictures.

"Jonathan saw his friends die; he fought for them and they for him. He loved them and told me about them in his letters. But when he came home all I saw was anger. Anger at his superiors for not protecting their men. Anger at the country for not having a clear picture of what they should be doing in Iraq. And anger toward the Army for threatening to make him stay in uniform. I didn't know it at the time, but Jonathan was looking for a way out. He'd gotten hurt during a mortar attack, and his back bothered him at night. Then it seemed like everything would hurt, and he started walking with a cane and asking if I could get him pain medication because the Army doctors wouldn't get it for him. I didn't know what to do other than help. So I went to my doctor and told him I was in pain. Then I shipped the pills to Jonathan."

She became quiet again, remembering.

"It wasn't until they kicked him out of the Army that I found out the whole story. The military police that had to escort him home gave me a piece of paper. It said that Jonathan was caught stealing from the base hospital and from the clinics. He was taking pills for himself and selling some to other soldiers. I told them they were wrong, that they had the wrong soldier. But the sergeant just shook his head and told me to talk to my son."

Rose set her tea on the small kitchen table, and then she walked over to the pictures of her son and took one from the wall.

"Some days I still can't believe it was him. He told me everything, that he'd lied to me to get the pills, that the pain would never go away, that he didn't care what anyone thought and that he wanted to die." She stroked the picture of her son and pinned it back on the wall. "He left not long after. Just disappeared one day while I was at work. All the money I had in the apartment was gone, along with some silver and a necklace my mother left me. I didn't care about the things, but..."

I understood. He'd returned home broken somehow. I'd seen it in others and I'd experienced it myself. Everyone copes in different ways. For some, the pain comes from the memories. For others, it comes from no longer being part of something. No matter how scary or awful it was, being with your fellow Marines or soldiers somehow made it better. When you left that safe haven and returned to the real world, it felt like you were floating through a never-ending cloud of indecision and obscurity, like no one knew you, and no one ever knew how to act around you. It was something I was still dealing with myself, as I watched Rose touch each and every picture of her son.

There were tears in her eyes now, and when she turned once again to face me, her eyes were swollen and tired.

"I started looking for him in every place I could. I wrote to the Army and to my congressman. I even talked to a state senator on the phone who made some calls to the VA. But nothing worked; my Jonathan was gone. So now I walk the streets asking people if they've seen him. I know how it must look, like I'm a crazy woman, but I'm not crazy." A sudden intensity flamed her words now. "I am his mother and I always will be. I feel him like he's still in me. I feel his pain and I know something is wrong."

I didn't ask how she knew it. I'd seen things in the past that couldn't be explained. Some were figments of people's imagination, and some might be called miracles or divinely inspired occurrences. It really didn't matter; I could see that she believed what she was saying with every ounce of her tortured soul.

But something was nagging at me, pushing me to inquire when maybe I should've just kept my mouth shut. I didn't.

"But why do you walk the streets? Couldn't he be anywhere?"

Her eyes sparkled like I'd just asked the magic question.

"I know he's here," she said. I could feel the conviction. I pressed further, not really knowing why.

"How do you know?"

Rose smiled for the first time and said, "His bank statements still come to this address. I see his disability money going in and he's still writing checks and making withdrawals."

Now things were getting weird. Why would her son stay in Seattle? The guy had to have turned into a real piece of work if that were the case. Or maybe there was another answer, a more uncomfortable one.

"How do you know it's him, Rose? Isn't it possible that someone stole his ATM card or got hold of his checkbook?"

She shook her head and smiled again like my questions would never upset her.

"I didn't tell you the most important part!"

I waited for her explanation, as if anything would make any real sense. I was starting to feel like maybe I just should've left her at the front door and gone on my way. But I'd be lying if I said my interest wasn't piqued. What would cause a son, who'd just gotten booted from the Army, most likely with a dishonorable discharge (maybe an other than honorable with a medical dispensation), to leave home but still stay in the same city where his mom lived? Seattle's a big place, but still. She had to be confused. I was afraid someone was taking advantage of her.

"How do you know he's here, Rose? How do you know he's still in Seattle?"

Rose's smile never wavered when she said, "He writes me letters!" And, as if to explain, she rushed to the kitchen, opened a drawer and withdrew a stack of white envelopes. She hurried back, thrusting them into my hands. "See! They're all there. My Jonathan just needs me to find him."

CHAPTER THREE

It took me twenty minutes to get through all the letters. They read more like a diary than letters home. Rose's son talked about his feelings, about how the world seemed to be collapsing around him; in some letters he'd had the odd sunny day. They were strange in a way that made me think he wasn't the one writing them. Maybe he was just high all the time. The handwriting was a bit muddled, but he could've grown up that way. I didn't know too many guys with neat handwriting.

Not one of the letters asked for money, and he never said where he was. But each envelope had a stamp identifying the place of origin as somewhere in the vicinity of Seattle. They varied, but I recognized most of the names from my limited experience in town.

When I finally looked up from the letters, Rose was waiting expectantly.

"See, I told you," she said, sounding like a toddler who'd just proved a point to her parents. The nagging feeling that Rose's mind wasn't quite right itched at my insides. Part of me wanted to run, to be as far away from whatever web her son had woven as I could. But the pleading in Rose's eyes stopped me. How could I abandon this woman to her misery? At least if I could help her find some answers maybe she could move on, and maybe then she could get the help she so clearly needed.

"Would you like me to help you find him?" I asked, not really believing that the words just came out of my mouth.

Rose's eyes lit up and she clapped her hands twice.

"That would be wonderful, just so wonderful. Thank you!" And then her face sagged a bit, and I wondered if she was drifting off to wherever her mind liked to wander. But she surprised me again when she said, "I am sorry. I've been so rude. Here I've been going on and on about my problems, and I don't even know your name."

It was hard not to smile at that.

"My name is Daniel. Daniel Briggs."

I LEFT Rose's apartment soon after, not fully comprehending what I'd just committed myself to. The letters and Rose's words banged around in my head as I walked toward Pike Place. Angelo might still be there, and I wanted to tell him everything was okay, even though he hadn't lifted a finger to help.

Part of me wondered if the young punks had come back looking for me. I wasn't worried, but I was concerned for Angelo. If the little runt and his friends were smart enough to put two and two together, they might just make trouble for my boss.

The streets were mostly deserted when I returned to the market. Angelo had apparently finished the cleanup and gone home. I'd have to wait until morning to check in.

So I waved to the guy driving the street sweeper as I

swung a right and headed home. He returned the wave with middling enthusiasm, always keeping his eyes on the curb that his machine was attempting to return to order.

The blocks passed by as I weaved my way through downtown. Groups of friends and couples walked by me, either on their way home or to one of the many bars around town. The city felt like it was buzzing with activity, and by the time I reached my own apartment, the electricity of the night had swung me far from sleep. I ignored the front door and kept walking, the breeze coming in from the Puget Sound acting as a welcome distraction.

Instead of thinking about Rose and her son, I started thinking about the other men and women who came home from war, battered and weary, some far more than others. America was still deep in a patriotic fervor for her troops, and while I didn't think that was a bad thing, I wondered where it might lead. I'd already seen fellow Marines take advantage of the situation, and I hoped the quiet epidemic wouldn't spread.

Those thoughts gripped me as I paced along, always keeping an eye on the shadows and the faces of strangers. With my hands tucked in my trouser pockets, I made myself as inconspicuous as possible – another old habit. It made me less of a target.

I passed a group of four homeless men chatting in a dimly lit alley. They were passing a bottle around, chuckling about something. They looked old and worn, and I wondered where they went when the temperatures dropped, with the cold Northwest winter blowing in from Siberia, or wherever it came from.

For some reason I stopped on the other side of the alley, something nagging in the recesses of my mind. I pulled out the picture Rose had given me, one of the many from her apartment shrine, showing Jonathan in full smile on his boot camp graduation day. It gave me an idea.

When I entered the alleyway, the four homeless guys became silent. Most people thought a drunk on the street was oblivious to what was going on around them, but in my experience they could be more skittish than a kitten in a dog kennel. These four were no different, and I saw them tuck the bottle away and take up varied familiar positions. It was like they were playing possum to come off as nonthreatening as possible, or maybe to appear less like targets.

"I'm sorry to bother you," I said, keeping my hands where they could see them. I raised the three by five photo in the air. "I was wondering if you would mind taking a look at this picture."

The four men exchanged looks. One of them asked, "What is it?"

"It's a friend," I answered, keeping my tone as nonthreatening as possible. "I'm looking for him and was wondering if you'd seen him."

Another look was shared among the companions before the man who'd asked the question rose from his makeshift mattress.

"Let me take a look."

He came closer and I could smell the booze on his breath as he moved in to get a better look. After a shower and a shave, I thought the man could've passed as a normal member of society. His voice was clear and only his eyes showed any hint that he'd been at the sauce for some time. I handed him the picture.

"Soldier?" he asked, pointing to the image.

I nodded.

He grunted and said, "Too bad." He shook his head. "Larry over there was in the Army, weren't you, Larry?"

One of the others grunted back, giving him a thumbs-up.

"You a soldier too?" the man asked.

"A Marine," I said.

The man looked at me and then back down at the picture.

"You mind if I show my friends?"

"I'd appreciate it if you did."

He sniffed and took the photo to his buddies. Every one of them gave the image a hard look, shaking their head, expressing what I realized was sadness. No doubt they'd encountered their fair share of lost souls like Rose's son, Jonathan.

"Sorry, kid," the man said, handing the picture back to me. "Hey, I just thought of something. There's a breakfast wagon run by some veterans. It's open every Sunday morning at six down by the Space Needle. Best muffins in town. Me and the boys never miss it. Maybe you should check it out."

It couldn't hurt. I didn't have to be at the market until seven, so maybe a quick pass would help.

"Thanks," I said, pocketing the picture. "Maybe I'll see you there."

The man gave me a crooked grin and then turned back to his friends. His good deed completed, he grabbed the brown paper-wrapped bottle from Larry and returned to the festivities.

THAT NIGHT I slept in fits. I kept seeing the hunched image of Rose wandering the streets of Seattle, passersby mocking her and occasionally throwing stones. As the night dragged on, Rose got older, until in the final dream she was barely shuffling along, her hair thin and gray, her eye sockets hollow, and all the excitement from earlier in the day gone forever.

My alarm woke me for the first time in ages. I never used an alarm. I didn't have to. Somehow my body knew when sunrise was coming. The battlefield had imprinted some otherworldly sense of self-preservation that would never go away. But that morning it did, and I'm not gonna lie, it spooked me.

After a quick shower, I slipped into one of seven identical work outfits consisting of heavy work pants and a plaid button-down shirt. Once my boots were tied, I slipped out into the morning, the air crisp and gray. It appeared to be any normal Pacific NW morning. A low fog felt like it was burning off, but in Seattle you never knew for sure.

The streets were mostly empty as I started my journey toward the world-famous Space Needle, a novelty to tourists and a hideous eyesore to some Seattleites. Angelo said it reminded him of a spaceship, and he once joked that it was a beacon for aliens. I didn't really care. Modern architecture held little interest to me, unless it helped me in finding the safest ingress and egress routes.

By the time I reached the Space Needle, there was a line twenty people long waiting for breakfast. The muffins, coffee and milk were being served on a trio of collapsible plastic tables where three men and a woman tended to their guests with respectful smiles. I didn't want to intrude, and I certainly wasn't there for the food, so I made my way past the line and waited by the van I surmised brought the charitable feast.

More homeless men and women trickled in, some pushing carts, others scooting along as if pulled by the smell of coffee. It was hard to watch the families, mostly mothers with small children, eyes wide at the sight of food. I tried not to think about them; it was best not to get involved.

Just as it looked like the food was dwindling, my old friends from the night before picked their way through the crowd and got in line. Larry, the old soldier, waved to me with a sloppy grin, and the man who had helped with Jonathan's picture held up a finger like he was coming right over.

After grabbing what was left of the muffins, he made his way to me, every fifth or sixth step a bit unsteady. He was blowing on his coffee when he finally got to me. Some of the beverage had sloshed over the side.

"Well hello, stranger," he said. "I see you found it."

"Yeah, thanks."

He wobbled a bit as his lips sought out the edge of the cup. "You find the boy you were looking for?"

"Not yet. I was waiting for them to finish handing out food."

He nodded and sipped his coffee. Then he stared at the cup for a moment, set his plate on the ground, and fished something out of his pocket. "Hair of the dog!" he said, twisting the top off the tiny liquor bottle with his teeth and poured some of it in his coffee.

This time when he sipped it, he smiled. "That's so much better."

By now Larry and the other two had joined us. They all looked to be in the same shape – tired and drunk. They crammed muffins into their mouths and nodded appreciatively, crumbs clinging to their unkempt beards and their stained shirts.

"You happen to know who's in charge here?" I asked.

Larry looked up this time and pointed with a gloved finger to the serving tables. "The young one, I think. The guy with the ball cap."

The helpers were packing things up, handing whatever was left to the homeless still eating. The guy Larry had pointed out made the effort to chat for a moment with each person he encountered. He couldn't have been much older than me. From what I observed, it looked like he genuinely cared. It made me wonder what inspired a young man to spend his Sundays on the streets serving food to veterans and the homeless. Surely he had a family, or at least a girlfriend.

He was dressed casually, in jeans, a black North Face sweater, and a ball cap. The cap had an American flag on it, bold and proud. When he'd given away his last muffin, the guy's eyes scanned the rest of the crowd, making sure no one had gone unnoticed. His gaze settled on me for a split second, shifted, and then snapped back. There was recognition in his eyes like he was silently asking me, "Don't I know you?" and then his eyes lit up.

"Holy shit!" he said, loud enough for some of those around him to look up from their meals. He didn't apologize but bee-lined for me. His intense enthusiasm made me want to back away because nowhere in my memory could I place the guy, but I stood my ground until he said, "Briggs, is that you?"

I must have put on an anxious half grin because he was quick to add, "You probably don't remember me. I'm Tanner Gray. I was with Bravo Company, One Eight."

I'd spent my entire career as a Marine with 1st Battalion Eighth Marines out of Camp Lejeune, first as an infantryman, and then as a scout sniper. There were a lot of memories in that unit, some good, some bad. I didn't want to think about it.

"Hey," I replied awkwardly.

Tanner spoke to the four homeless men I'd met the night before saying, "Did you know that Sergeant Daniel *Snake Eyes* Briggs was the best bad-ass sniper I've ever seen, maybe that anyone's ever seen? Man, I remember this one time my company was pinned down by enemy mortar fire. We couldn't get anyone on the radio except for old Snake Eyes. So we're waiting and waiting, and the next thing you know, we hear six rifle shots, and then the mortars went quiet. My platoon commander sent my squad to check it out, and hell if I didn't find Snake Eyes and his spotter standing over six guys and three mortar tubes. One shot apiece. All dead."

Tanner's audience stared at me with a mixture of awe and confusion. I kept my mouth shut, willing the raging emotion in the pit of my stomach to subside. It had been rare that I'd ever bumped into anyone from my time in the Corps. I wished it would never happen, and I hadn't kept in touch with anyone for that very reason. The images were too real, the smells still clung to my senses. It wasn't the killing. It was never that. Killing was easy, especially when the enemy was trying to kill you, but the regrets were what haunted me in the darkest reaches of the night, like ghouls reaching out their crumbling hands to claim me.

Tanner was still going on.

"Hell, the last time I'd heard the Marine Corps was going to award him with..."

I felt my eyes go cold, the Beast shooting daggers at Tanner Gray. He saw it, probably even felt it, because his mouth hung slack for a moment, before it closed slowly. Then he recovered.

"Anyway, a lot of us owe Briggs a huge debt."

My chest was still thumping, but my breath returned. Tanner and I stared at each other, he was probably waiting for my outburst and I, well, I didn't know what to say. Then my real purpose in visiting snapped back into place. I pulled out the picture of Rose's son and handed it to Tanner.

"I was wondering if you or any of your helpers have seen this guy."

Tanner looked at the picture thoughtfully.

"I haven't, but maybe someone else has. You mind if I show them?"

I shook my head and Tanner went to show the rest of the volunteers. There was no recognition in their eyes. Tanner was nice enough to make his way around to the other home-less guests and ask them as well. None could remember ever seeing the young man, and when Tanner returned, he apologized.

"Thanks for checking," I said.

"No problem."

I heard a squealing and turned to see a huge pickup truck, lifted with enormous tires, chugging toward us.

"Dammit, I told him not to bring that thing," Tanner said, putting up his hands to tell the driver to slow down. He got a long honk in response, and when the monster truck came to a stop, the driver stuck his left hand out the window and gave Tanner the middle finger. "That's my little brother," Tanner said, his voice a bit strained.

I didn't know what to make of Tanner's brother. They looked like twins, but when the younger Gray hopped down from his mighty steed, I saw the swagger right away. He was dressed head to toe in woodland camouflage, the kind hunters wear, not the military camouflage. The chew in his mouth was overflowing, and he spat a steaming gob of juice onto the sidewalk.

Some of the homeless were pointing and murmuring, and I think this made Tanner walk faster.

I only heard snippets of their conversation, but it was plain that Tanner was trying to relay to his brother that rolling up acting like a first-class redneck was not something you did when feeding the hungry. There was a halfhearted shrug from his brother, a sigh from Tanner, and then the two made their way over to me.

"Daniel Briggs, I'd like you to meet my little brother, Aaron Gray. Baby Aaron is a fellow Marine who likes to take his redneckery to the next level."

Aaron Gray gave me a yellow-toothed smile, stuck out a meaty hand and said, "Dishonorable discharge at your service, Jarhead."

I shook his hand and smiled. At least he was honest. But I

didn't really like the look in his eyes, like he was ready to pick a fight no matter the reason. I'd met tough guys like him before, guys who'd spit in your face and call you a pansy just to get you to take a swing first.

I didn't say a thing and thankfully Tanner interjected before his brother could make another smart ass comment. Not that I would've taken the bait, but I didn't have time to listen.

"You gonna give us a hand cleaning up or what?" Tanner asked his brother.

Aaron Gray shrugged but followed his brother to the tables. I was about to turn and go when Tanner came back and handed me something. It was the picture of Rose's son. I'd completely forgotten about it.

"Thanks," I said, pocketing the photo before my suddenly distracted mind could do it harm.

"I wish I could've helped more," he said. He looked like he meant it. "Hey, if you're not busy tonight, could I buy you a beer and maybe catch up on old times?"

Every fiber of my body wanted me to say no. I didn't need the reminder of my past life. Bumping into Tanner had been bad enough. Sitting around drinking and reliving the glory days sounded like torture. Since I was anything but rude, I said, "Sure. I get off at eight."

"Where do you work?"

"Angelo's, down at Pike Place."

"Cool. I'll come by at eight."

I nodded and made my way past Larry and the others. They were still staring, but I waved to them anyway. When I checked for traffic before crossing the street, my eyes swept back to the van that was now fully loaded, the crowd filled for another Sunday. Tanner was getting into the driver's seat, but that wasn't what caught my eye. There, leaning against the hood of the van was Aaron Gray, cell phone pressed to his ear, with his eyes locked on me. He didn't look away when our eyes met, but he did grin and give me a little salute with two fingers. I nodded and went on my way, tempted to pull out the old quarter that always sat in my pocket. One flip and my choice would be made. Maybe it was time to leave town...maybe.

CHAPTER FOUR

The rest of the day was no different than so many others. Fish. Ice. Sweep. Over and over I went, my concentration hard on my task, my mind elsewhere.

I thought about Rose and her son, who was probably dead or working toward that end goal. I thought about Tanner Gray and his brother Aaron, two Marines who couldn't be any more different. Then I thought about myself, and how I'd somehow landed in Seattle and found a measure of peace. Only now I was pulled into drama again, however slight, yet drama nonetheless.

I wanted to be free of adventure and pain. A quiet life beckoned with the irresistible call of a Pied Piper. I wanted to follow that calling, settle down in a cozy nook far off the grid, maybe raise some livestock, but then again maybe not. I didn't need much. What the government sent me for my time in was enough. I even had some friends who might want some help in exchange for a modest living.

My options swished and swayed as I swept the floors, squeegeed the tile, and hauled Angelo's fish. This had been a nice stop, a place to get a peek at a different life, but it wasn't my home, not by a long shot. Angelo had been good to me, even kind, but his actions, or lack of action, the night before with the punks who'd accosted Rose, made me want to hand in my notice.

I didn't do that. Instead, I ignored Angelo's gaze, kept my head down, and kept thinking. I was always thinking.

TANNER GRAY SHOWED up just as eight o'clock tolled. He had a carefree air about him that made it seem like he was floating. I was a bit jealous of that fact, and I wondered how different my life could've been if I'd followed the same path as Tanner.

We shook hands and decided to grab a quick bite. We headed to one of Tanner's favorite bars, a dive called Chappy's, a few blocks away. It took a few minutes, but as Tanner chatted away, I felt myself falling into the same old rhythm; me the listener while my fellow Marine spun his tales. He was a good storyteller, and the way he remembered events, cleverly delivering lines like a stand-up comedian, made me remember my days in the Corps with affection for possibly the first time in years. We talked about the changes that happen, and how military service was a funny thing. Before you go to boot camp, you're charged up about serving your country. Some guys get tattoos and then get shit about it when their drill instructors see them without a shirt on.

Then, in boot camp, the only thing you want is for it to be over. You share comments with your fellow recruits like, "It'll be different when we get to the fleet," or "They'll treat us differently as soon as we get to SOI (School of Infantry)."

Your MOS (Military Occupational Specialty) school comes and goes, and then you finally get to the fleet, and once again you're a boot. Again you are at the bottom, a nobody, a green private or PFC ripe for whatever working party the corporals and sergeants have to fill. You make your way up in rank, always griping with your buddies, even mouthing off to sergeants at times, and as you get closer to getting out, it's all you can think about. That's the way the majority of Marines are, and don't let anyone tell you different.

Tanner and I laughed at the memory, even if that hadn't been the way it was for me. I loved being a sniper at war. The adventure was thrilling, and the ability to save an entire platoon with a single bullet was an addiction that kept me going back for more. Even that night, the nightmares of loss still fresh in my mind, some part of me longed for that simplicity, because that was what it had been for me. Simple. *Kill or be killed.*

Before I knew it, we'd polished off a fair amount of beer, and the clock on the wall said midnight. It was the first alcohol I'd consumed in months, and even though I felt the warmth within me, I did not feel the need to continue drinking. I switched to water and Tanner followed suit.

"What time do you go to work?" he asked.

"Nine o'clock on Mondays."

"Lucky bastard. It's seven on the nose for me and that's after a forty-minute drive in."

We hadn't broached the subject of work until then. Funny how that topic is shelved when you get to talking about old times.

"What do you do?" I asked, genuinely curious, seeing as how I'd never had a real job after leaving the Corps.

"I work for the VA," he sat up straight and twitched his nose like he was someone important. "I am an entry-level claims specialist," he said importantly, even pretending like he was tightening an invisible bow tie at his neck.

I chuckled and asked, "What the hell does that mean?"

He dropped the silly facade and asked, "You ever have to deal with the VA?"

"A little." My platoon sergeant had actually had to march me to the local Veterans Affairs office before I got out. That was how I was drawing disability, even though at the time, and sometimes even now, I didn't think I deserved it. But Gunny O'Neill had been firm, "You'll need this, Briggs," he'd said. "And besides, you deserve it." After some shrink had asked me a bunch of questions, they'd given me my claim number. All it took after that was my John Hancock on some papers.

"So I'm the first contact that Marines, sailors, soldiers, whoever, come to see when they think they have a claim. Now that we've been at war for a few years, the number of claims is really going up. I'm one of five people they just brought on to handle the workload." I knew it had gotten bad, and it seemed like every time I happened to see the news there was another report on the number of wounded veterans coming home or the number of Marines committing suicide.

"That's gotta be hard work."

"It's okay. I mean, it sure beats getting shot at. And anyway, I feel like I'm doing some good, you know, like I'm giving back."

You had to respect that. To some it might've just been a job, but to Tanner it seemed to be much more.

"Is that how you started to do the Sunday breakfast thing?"

"Believe it or not, that was my brother's idea. He was joking about homeless vets one night. I think he was pretty stoned at the time, and he dared me to do it." Tanner laughed. "That was six months ago and we haven't missed one Sunday yet."

"Where do you get the money from?" I couldn't imagine

an entry-level claims specialist made enough money to fund the outreach program, no matter how humble.

"We all chip in a little, and sometimes we get money from wealthy donors who have plenty of dough to spare. It's a win-win really. They get to feel good about giving to the vets, and we get to help those in need."

"So, you do all the grunt work?" I asked, the rare joke leaving my lips before I even realized it.

Tanner laughed. "Yeah. I guess you can take a grunt out of the Corps, but you can never take the grunt out of the grunt."

We shared another laugh and then Tanner's face became serious.

"Look, I know it's none of my business, but if you ever need a favor down at the VA, or even someone to talk to, all you need to do is ask."

"Thanks," I said, trying to keep my unease from showing. Tanner's smile was back, like the comment was forgotten. It was a nice gesture and one I wouldn't forget. But if he thought I was really going to talk to another shrink again, he had no idea who I was.

WE SAID our goodbyes and I promised to call if I needed anything. Tanner said he'd stop by Angelo's if he had a chance, and when I headed back toward my apartment, it felt like one of those "forever" farewells. It wasn't that I didn't enjoy his company, but my life was headed in another direction, and this had merely been another in a series of brief interludes that marked my chosen path.

It was time to leave. I knew that now. I didn't need to flip a coin or take time to think about it because the die had already been cast. Some might call it running, but I called it moving on. It was something I did well; the road was all I knew now.

I would say goodbye to Rose and wish her well in her search. Maybe I'd even make a phone call or two, inherently placing the task of finding Jonathan on some other person's to-do list. My list was full. It had everything to do with finding my own peace and my own selfish wish to be alone and happy, in my own way.

Plans stacked up before me as I trudged along, each step closer to my inevitable exit. I was so consumed with my impending leave of absence that when I turned the final corner before hitting the front door of my apartment complex, I almost ran into the hooded figures looking directly at my destination. They turned in unison and I immediately recognized one face before it said with a sneer, "Get him, boys."

CHAPTER FIVE

Somehow the runt and his three friends, accompanied by two reinforcements, had found me. It took me less than a second to guess that Angelo either gave them my address of his own volition, or that they'd gotten it out of him using either physical threats or acts of violence. That answer would have to wait for later, as a silver pistol flashed in front of my face.

I didn't think, my body moving before my brain had a beat to catch up. I pivoted like I was going to run, but as I did, my left arm whipped across, my torso's momentum giving it maximum power. My hand clamped over the gun, and I felt the gunman squeeze the trigger. The bullet slammed into the brick wall next to my head; luckily my head was down or I would have received a face full of brick shrapnel.

I kept turning, the gun pried out of the falling man's hand as his own face followed the trajectory of the bullet and crashed into the wall. I sensed, more than I saw, him crumple to the ground. My momentum already had me spinning in a circle, going low this time, with the pistol twisted around in my hand. Butt end first, the weapon slammed into the knee of my second target. The man howled in pain and toppled over. He managed to hold onto his own pistol, although I promptly stomped it out of his hand, eliciting another blood-curdling scream from the would-be gunman.

I was standing up now, facing the four young hoods, a gun in one hand and my other hand tightly balled into a fist. My inner Beast grinned and my own face matched his mirth. I wanted to let it out, to tear into the four, exacting the revenge the Beast wanted.

But something stopped me. It wasn't the fact that I was still outnumbered, or the fact the Beast had calmed, but it was the look in the four boys' eyes. I registered their fear. Real fear, visceral and unbidden.

"Who the hell are you, man?" the runt asked. He was backing away slowly, apparently unconcerned about the two men lying on the ground.

I didn't answer, but I did take another step forward. This action caused an immediate reaction with all four boys stumbling backward.

"Go home," I said, my words sounding more like a growl.

The runt nodded and pointed to the men on the ground.

"Take them with you," I said, "But leave the gun."

Another quick nod and the runt was ordering his underlings to pick up the fallen reinforcements. They hurried on their way, somehow dragging the unconscious man, whose nose was definitely broken, and the moaning man with the crushed knee, down 1st Avenue.

I waited first one minute and then two more. My heart slowed from a steady staccato to its normal calm rhythm. To my surprise, I heard no police sirens. I wondered if the neighborhood was just used to clamming up when danger came calling. I hadn't seen or heard any violence during my stay in

Seattle, but I was new, so maybe I was just unaware of perti-
nent history.

After five minutes of waiting, I pocketed both pistols
and started walking. I didn't want to enter my apartment.
There wasn't much there of value anyway. My only valuables
were locked safely in a bank, closer to the heart of downtown, the only mementos I'd brought on my never-ending
journey.

But I didn't get far. Just after passing my building, I heard
clapping. I turned and looked toward the shadows. There was
no one in plain sight until a moment later when a figure
stepped out from underneath an awning, still clapping.

"Nice show you put on there," the man said. It was Aaron
Gray, Tanner's brother.

"What are you doing here?" I asked, slipping my hands
into my pockets.

Aaron put his own hands into the air, demonstrating he
meant no harm. Then, ever so slowly, he lowered his own
hand behind his head, and came out holding a sawed-off shotgun. I tensed, but Aaron kept the shotgun pointed in the air.

"I thought you might need some help," he said, chewing
on his cheek full of tobacco.

"How did you know?"

He pointed to the weapon in his hand as if to ask if he
had permission to put it down. I nodded and he came closer,
the shotgun now hanging at his side.

"A call went out late last night. Said the Pier Sixty-Two
Crew was looking for someone that matched your description. I put two and two together, and here I am."

I stared at the younger Gray, wondering if it had just been
coincidence, or if maybe he'd come for whatever reward
might have been offered. He guessed what I was thinking and
answered my question.

"I might not have been the most squared-away Marine,

but I'll be damned if I let a bunch of hoods take out one of my brothers."

I didn't know what to say. This guy didn't know me, yet there was the inexplicable bond that centuries of Marines before us had cultivated and bred in subsequent generations. I remember an old Marine buddy telling me that even the biggest shit bag in the Corps stood a little straighter when he marched past a group of soldiers or airmen. It was a strange thing, even though I'd seen it myself in the past. But it seemed so out of place on the dark streets of Seattle that I couldn't help but be skeptical.

"Well, thanks," I managed to say.

"Don't mention it," Aaron replied, even though he really hadn't lifted a finger to help. "You need a lift somewhere? My truck is around the corner."

"I'm good."

What I needed was some time to think until morning came when I could retrieve my things from the bank. After tonight's turn of events, it appeared the place where I worked and the place where I lived were no longer safe for me to return. I wasn't one to run from a fight, but at that moment it seemed like such a hassle. I was tired of the fighting, and the weapons in my pockets seemed to weigh a thousand pounds. They were tools I was intimately familiar with, that had once kept me safe, but now they felt like anchors chaining me to where I stood.

"Could you do me a favor?"

Aaron seemed surprised by the question, but he nodded.

"Could you take care of these for me?" I pulled out the two pistols and held them out.

He was a gun nut and eagerly took them.

"Not a problem," he said, checking to see that the weapons were loaded and each safety was on.

I nodded my thanks and went on my way.

"Let me know if you find any more weapons. I'm happy to take them off your hands!"

I heard him laugh out loud over my shoulder, but I didn't turn back. I had to find a place to rest, and then I'd leave.

I STAYED the night in a cheap motel in a seedy part of town. They rented rooms by the hour, but luckily I'd withdrawn some cash prior to the night's events. The cashier grinned from his perch behind iron bars in the lobby and happily took my one hundred dollars.

Despite needing the rest, I couldn't sleep. I tossed and turned, replaying the day in my head, wondering where I'd gone wrong. I worried about what my actions might cost Rose and even Angelo. In the end, I knew I couldn't leave, not yet.

So, when the first rays of dawn came in through the rumpled curtains, I got up from the uncomfortable bed and left the motel. My first stop would be Pike Place, where I knew Angelo would already be working, dealing with the fish suppliers who brought in their daily catch.

I was right. As soon as I arrived, Angelo looked up from where he was haggling with an older gentleman who supplied Angelo with squid and urchin. I winced when I saw Angelo's face. His lip was split and one eye was swollen shut.

Angelo finished his haggling and handed over a wad of cash to the fisherman. I joined him, and we started unloading the day's supply.

"Are you okay?" I asked.

"Yes."

He grunted as a he lifted an urchin-laden basket onto the dolly.

"Was it the guys from yesterday?"

"It was." He stopped what he was doing, and his face

twisted like he wanted to say something. Then he shook his head and resumed working.

"I came to tell you that I'm leaving."

Angelo stopped again, this time his head drooped as he turned to face me.

"I am sorry for yesterday," he said, his Italian accent thick now. "I was scared. I shouldn't have told you not to help that poor lady."

He thought I didn't understand, but I did. Normal people cower in the face of bullies. It's only natural, and it's the reason some bullies make the best criminals while others become rich and powerful in skyscraper corporations. Angelo was a salt-of-the-Earth type of guy, a man who'd made his own way through toil and struggle.

"I'm not mad, Angelo, and it's not your fault I'm leaving."

"No, but I should have helped. You were only being—"

I put up my hand to stop him.

"It's not your fault, I promise. I've just got some other things to take care of. We both knew this was a short-term gig anyway."

"I will bring you to the front, give you a raise."

It was a kind gesture, but one he could ill afford. His business ran on slim margins, and I wasn't about to take them.

"Thank you, but no. I'll finish up today, and then I'll be on my way."

I was true to my word, and despite repeated attempts by Angelo, and even his other employees, to get me to stay, I said my goodbyes as soon as the nightly closing finished.

Angelo escorted me out, locking the storeroom behind us.

"Thanks for everything, Angelo. I sincerely mean it."

"No. Thank you, Daniel. You have reminded me what courage looks like." He reached out a gnarled hand and I took it. "Here," he said, producing a rubber-banded roll of cash from his opposite hand. "Your final paycheck and a little extra for the road."

I was going to reject it, but I could see that Angelo wasn't going to take no for an answer. So I stuffed the cash in my pocket and went on my way.

I HAD one more night to wait. By working my last day in Seattle, I'd missed my chance to pick up my belongings from the bank safety deposit box. Part of me wanted to leave then, but the seemingly worthless baubles in that box still held meaning for me.

So I headed back to the same motel I'd stayed in the night before, and the cashier from the night before sat behind the same security grate in the lobby. But this time he had the gall to ask for one hundred twenty dollars. I held out, understanding that he was probably pocketing at least half of the rent. He acquiesced, and I got another dingy room, another lumpy bed, with the same paper thin walls.

DESPITE MY EXHAUSTION from the night before, sleep came in spurts, my dreams frenzied and always the same. I had a dream about Rose, drowning in a sea of tears, somehow being pulled in as her mouth opened to an unnatural size, a silent scream caught in her throat. As she drowned, I saw a face below the water, ghost-like and smiling. It was her son Jonathan, his eyes a burning red, as he devoured the drowning body of his mother.

MORNING CAME AND, once again, I made my way out of the hotel. Three hookers were in the lobby chatting away on cell phones. One of them flashed me on the way out, apparently trying to get one last gig before she headed to bed to sleep. I ignored them and hit the street, my destination set.

Nothing would stop me now. A quick visit to the bank to get my belongings, and then it was off to the bus station, or maybe the train station. There was something soothing about trains, whereas buses always seemed to smell like baby vomit and piss.

I walked across town, once stopping for a cup a coffee and later for a donut at a packed bakery. I had some time to kill before the bank opened so I spent my final morning taking in Seattle through the eyes of a tourist. I enjoyed taking in one last view before boarding a train to places unknown.

My thoughts were of solitude again, peace and quiet, far away from the hustle of the city. From a bus stop bench I watched office workers, bellmen and mothers pushing babies. I came to the realization that they were all heading somewhere while I seemed to be headed nowhere. The truth of that fact hit me hard. I'd made a promise to Rose to help her find her son, but at the first sign of discomfort I was cutting and running.

Something deep within told me that wasn't who I was; I'd been trained to do better, to keep my promises, no matter the cost. I shifted in my seat, suddenly uncomfortable with sitting still. The bank would be open in fifteen minutes. Maybe a little more walking would calm me.

But as I took those first steps toward the bank, my legs protested every step. It seemed my body was rebelling, forcing me do the right thing. My chest tightened and I found it hard to take a breath. I stopped and looked up at the cloud-filled sky. It felt like rain, but what I really needed was air, sweet cool air to calm me, to fill my lungs, to give me the energy to leave Seattle.

All I felt was the increasing heat of the day punctuated by the rising blood to my face, like every step closer to the bank, away from my original mission, was drawing me closer to a heart attack. I took a step back and the pain eased. I took another step, and I could breathe again. One step further, and the pressure in my chest dulled to a subtle pinch.

I heaved a reluctant sigh and made my way back the way I'd come. It seemed that the universe, or maybe just my conscience, wasn't going to let me depart that easily. It was time to talk to Rose and get some answers.

ROSE ANSWERED her apartment door after asking who was there. I told her it was Daniel, and then waited for a few moments before I heard her undoing the collection of locks from the inside. She didn't open the door right away, but instead she peered out cautiously.

"Hello, Daniel."

"Hello, Rose."

She still wouldn't let me in. That was strange, but I took it as part of her cagey personality, another symptom in her alternate reality.

"May I come in?" I asked politely, not wanting to push her, but still feeling the need to press the issue.

Again the hesitation danced upon her face, like she was just meeting me for the first time. Finally, she nodded and opened the door wide.

I stepped inside and was once again greeted by the familiar scent of mint and bitter tea. There was a pot of water on the stove and steam was whistling violently out of the spout.

"I think your water's ready," I said.

Rose glanced over like she'd completely forgotten about the steaming pot. It made me wonder if she ever left the stove on for hours at a time. Should she really be living alone in her state?

She left the pot where it was after shutting off the gas burner. There she stood, not saying anything, her body tense, and her eyes locked on mine. I didn't know what she expected. I was there to get more information, but her body language made it seem like I was there to harass her. It was best to remove that notion.

"I came by to see if you'd remembered anything else, and I was hoping to take another look at the letters," I said.

"Letters?" Rose asked.

"Yes, the ones from Jonathan."

Rose's lips pursed, like she was trying to keep them from opening. She even slapped a hand over her mouth.

"Rose, is everything okay?"

She nodded, but her eyes widened with fear, like a frightened animal about to be beaten.

I tried to get closer, but she backed away.

"Did I say something—" I never got to finish. There was a crashing sound behind me, and suddenly there were two black masked forms bearing down. I never had a chance. I saw the Billy club coming, and my arm felt like it was moving through molasses as I tried to block the hit. I felt the blow on the side of my head. From that point on, there was only darkness.

CHAPTER SIX

The pounding in my head sounded like a sledge hammer crashing into the side of a semitrailer. Over and over it crashed, my head ringing as I floated through dark nothingness. There was no smell at first, and the thought that maybe I was dead crossed my addled senses.

The crashes slowed and then the pain came. I don't know how long it took me to realize that it wasn't a sound, but rather a feeling I was experiencing. Then it took more time to realize the feeling was a sharp pain in my head, behind my eyes and even in my neck. But if I was dead, how could I feel pain? Did you feel pain when you were dead? Or was I in some in-between place where you still felt remnants of human life while your body and mind made the transition to wherever your soul was sent?

I waited patiently, and through the pain I grabbed onto the only thing I could: hope. I hoped that it was all over, the bad dreams would finally be at an end. I hoped my travels would be over. I hoped the worries and regrets were gone forever, lost in the ether that I certainly was now passing through.

Hope, I thought. *I hope. I hope. I...*

That's when the sound returned. Not the pounding, but a voice, very close and urgent. I don't know how I even knew it was a voice. At that moment it sounded like I was hearing it underwater, like when you play those games as a kid and try to make your friends guess what you're saying at the bottom of the pool.

Strange. So very strange.

I listened hard, past the pain and despite my worry. There it was again but now with more insistence, like someone was calling me. But my mind continued to swirl through nothingness. I wanted to sleep forever. Forever sleep...

Then there were the slow beginnings of cold, or did it happen all of a sudden? I couldn't tell. It was like my nerve endings were running beats behind real time. Not that I knew what real time was, but there was a delay. There it was again, the cold washing over my face, like a dip in a frigid stream or when you dunked your head in an ice bucket full of apples. I'd done that once, and my mind drifted to the blurry image of me at age nine, bobbing for apples, a stem in my teeth as I grinned...

And then it was gone, replaced by more pain, and that sound again. *What was it?* I listened, trying to ignore the intense pain.

D...

I heard that for sure. I tried harder.

Daaaa...

Was it another memory?

Daaaanieeeeel.

The word was strung out, and I tried to wrap it tight in my head. *What was that word?* Was it just my imagination, or maybe it was the sound of the wind or passing clouds? At that moment, I wished I could see. Was I missing the untold beauty of the afterlife? Because other than the acute pain in my head, the rest of me felt euphoric. There were no more cares. The weight had been lifted.

For the first time in ages, I didn't care anymore, and the resulting freedom coursed through my veins like a salve, soothing me, singing its sweet lullaby.

Daannnieeel.

There it was again. I had to ignore it. It started to make me a little angry until I realized that whatever place I was in didn't allow anger. There was only the darkness, cool and comforting. The darkness...

Daniel!

The name cut into me like a spear, piercing my dreamlike state and jolting me away from the fading darkness. This time I really did focus, and as I did, other sensations returned. I don't know why I did. Maybe it was the pain that seemed as persistent as the name that was being whispered into my brain.

Then there was more pain, this time in what I remembered was my shoulder, searing, biting pain, like a hot poker.

Daniel!

It sounded like a hiss.

Daniel, wake up. Daniel.

Who was Daniel? That was a name, wasn't it?

Daniel. Hurry, I can't carry you like this.

Daniel. Was I Daniel?

As lazily as I could, I opened my eyes. Shapes danced in front of my vision, and I smiled at the kaleidoscope of colors. They were gray and hazy, but they looked beautiful, like a tapestry made just for me. My smile grew and I tried to reach out for the swirling picture, but my arms wouldn't move.

I decided to go back to sleep, and I closed my eyes again.

This time a stinging pain on my cheek brought me back, and when my eyes jolted open, there was something circular in my vision. It wobbled to and fro, and this time I found that I could reach out with my hands.

I clasped onto the object, trying to hold it steady. It was hairy on top, like a grass- covered ball, but the ball was hard, yet smooth, yet...

"Daniel, can you hear me?"

Daniel. I was Daniel.

"Whaaa?" I heard myself croak, even though it didn't sound like me.

"Shh, don't... I'm going to...you...hold on...outside..."

It sounded like a static-filled radio, the voice going in and out.

Then I felt my body being lifted, and then it was moving, and when I looked down, I saw my bare feet scraping along the ground. I wanted to laugh and I pointed to them, grinning. It was so interesting. I could've watched them forever.

The voice next to my head kept whispering. "Not much farther...hold...when I...night out...quiet..."

I tried to piece the words together, like someone was telling me a rhyme where all the words were jumbled and my muddled mind had to rearrange the words. Maybe something was wrong with my ears. I reached for my left ear and tugged. It was still there. So strange that the sound kept going in and out.

There was a creaking sound, and then I felt my toes thump over something hard and cold. The voice was quiet now, and as we moved, me and my muted companion, I tried to put the pieces together. But nothing worked, and at some point later, I gave up and went back to sleep.

THE NEXT TIME I sputtered to consciousness, my head was pounding. I put a tentative hand to my forehead and was relieved to find that I could actually make my body parts move.

I heard rustling and started to sit up, but fell back as my head swooned and the tendrils of unconsciousness almost reclaimed me.

"You should take it easy," said someone.

I resisted the urge to whirl around, afraid of what the sudden movement might do.

"Who's there?" I asked, my voice barely above a whisper. My mouth felt like it had been filled with salt and left to dry.

"It's Tanner Gray."

Tanner Gray? It took a couple of breaths to remember.

Right. The guy from 1/8. He has a brother named Aaron.

I couldn't remember ever feeling so fuzzy. Even during my deepest binges I'd never lost my memory this bad.

"What happened to me?"

"What's the last thing you remember?"

I heard Tanner coming closer, and I eased my eyes open. There was a shadowy blur in the corner of my vision, and it took a few blinks before the picture cleared.

But my memory was still hazy at best, and it took considerable effort to download my last recollection.

"I went to visit someone...and then there were two guys, and...that's all I remember."

Tanner sat down next to me on what I now realized was a pull-out sofa bed.

"Do you remember where they took you?"

I shook my head, immediately regretting the decision. It throbbed like waves lapping against the shore in a steady rhythm.

"Do you have anything for a headache?"

Tanner got up and went looking. He was back a minute later with a glass of water and a couple of pills.

I popped the pills in my mouth and downed the water like

I had not had water in years. Tanner took the glass and refilled it. I chugged the next one down, followed closely after yet another glass.

My stomach churned a bit, and the fourth glass I slowly sipped.

"Better?" Tanner asked.

"I will be after those pills kick in. Where the hell did you find me?"

Tanner frowned. "I think it's better I show you, once you're back on your feet."

I wanted answers, and was about to press harder, but whatever mule kick I'd gotten to my head returned me to reeling.

"Okay."

I DON'T KNOW when I fell asleep. When I awoke, Tanner was watching the news and was clicking away on a laptop perched on a pillow.

Grateful that my head was only slightly aching now, I eased myself into a sitting position, moving my hands and feet to make sure everything still worked. I winced when I tried to move my arms. My shoulder was stiff, and I touched it with my opposite hand. There was a bandage there, and when my hand moved down my arm, I noticed another bandage at the bend.

"Sorry about the shoulder," Tanner said, putting his laptop aside. "It was the only thing that would wake you up. You were pretty out of it."

"What did you do?"

He pulled something silver out of his pocket. It was a pen.

"You stabbed me?"

Tanner shrugged. "It was all I could think of."

I was about to uncork a deluge of questions, but his phone rang before I could choose where to begin.

"Yeah," Tanner said, putting up his finger for me to wait. "Sure, thanks." He ended the call. "That was work. I called in sick."

"What time is it?"

"One o'clock."

"PM?"

Tanner nodded.

How had I lost a whole day?

"I need to go," I said, easing my feet over the side of the sofa bed. Thankfully, this time the room didn't start spinning.

"I don't think that's a good idea."

"Why not?"

"It's not safe."

I was tired of all the riddles.

"What are you not telling me?"

Tanner took a few seconds to decide what to disclose before he said, "Look, you were kidnapped and taken to a really bad place, okay? Can you at least give me the day to see what I can find out?"

"I don't have time. Someone's expecting me."

"This thing isn't good, man. It's really not safe for you to be out on the streets, especially in your condition."

My condition. What exactly was my condition?

"Tanner, you've got exactly thirty seconds to explain to me what the hell is going on or I'm leaving through that door."

Tanner looked uncomfortable before saying, "What if I told you that I know who's behind your kidnapping? That they have the person you're trying to help?"

Rose!

"What are you talking about? How do you know?"

Tanner ran a hand through his hair, avoiding my gaze.

"It's my brother. It was Aaron who kidnapped you."

CHAPTER SEVEN

"What? But I just saw him," I said. I could still see him in my mind, standing under the lamppost, holding a shotgun in the air. "How do you know for sure?"

"I overheard him talking on the phone. He mentioned your name so I followed him."

"Followed him where?"

"To a warehouse."

I didn't remember a warehouse. Was that really where I'd woken up?

"How did you find me?"

"I snuck in after they left, and when I'd searched through the others—"

"What others?" My temper was ready to snap.

"It's hard to explain. I was hoping to show you."

"Would you just spit it out, dammit? What others?"

"You weren't the only one, Daniel. There were a lot more."

I almost asked a lot more what, but then it dawned on me. He was talking about other people. Was his brother kidnapping people? I mean, the guy looked like Mr. Sketchy

Sketcherson. Was it just a show the other night when he said he was there to help me with The Pier 62 Crew?

And, then I realized that Tanner had said *a lot more*.

"Who does he have in that warehouse, Tanner?" I asked through gritted teeth. I knew the answer even before he said it.

"I think they're all military veterans."

IT TOOK Tanner thirty minutes to tell me what he knew. He said he'd suspected his brother of being into some pretty illegal things, but that the episode at the warehouse showed him things were much worse than he'd feared.

"I knew he was into drugs and maybe some hustles, but that warehouse..." Tanner shivered.

"What did you see?"

"There were rows upon rows of cots. You know the olive drab with metal frames like we had in the Marines?"

I nodded. During my service, those cots had been a luxury. Most times it was either an ISO mat, if you were lucky, or the hard ground every other day. Cots weren't something you lugged around when you were hunting the enemy.

"How many?"

"I'd say probably around one hundred, maybe more."

I tried to imagine the scene, still concerned that I had zero recollection of actually being in that room except for our hasty exit. I didn't get it.

"How did we get out if there were that many people inside? Didn't someone see us?"

Tanner shook his head slowly, sadly even.

"No one saw us."

"How is that possible? Were they all—?"

The words caught in my throat. Had I been left for dead?

Tanner must have sensed what I was thinking because he was quick to add, "They weren't dead. They were asleep."

"Asleep?" I asked with incredulity.

"Everyone was hooked up to IV bags, and catheters, I think. I didn't have long to look around."

I touched the bandage on my arm and then ripped it off. There it was, a raised dimple with a pinprick of red in the center, right where they always took my blood.

"What was in the IV bags?" I asked, my fears bubbling just beneath the surface.

"I don't know, but whatever it is, it was enough to keep you and a hundred others out cold."

I remembered the lazy floating feeling, and the lack of pain or any real sensory input.

"Tell me where it is."

"I'll show you tonight."

"No. We need to go *now*."

"They'll be looking for you," Tanner said.

"I don't care." I was already on my feet, searching for my shoes. "Where are my shoes?"

"You didn't have any on when I found you."

The memory of my feet dragging on the floor came back to me then, and I wondered in what other ways I'd been violated.

"So do you have a car?"

"Yeah."

"Come on. I need to buy some new shoes."

OUR FIRST STOP was at the bank where I'd been headed the day before. Tanner let me out and I padded into the branch in the flip flops he'd loaned me.

After explaining to the manager that my wallet had been stolen, I had to fill out and sign forms to verify my identity.

The manager escorted me back to the safety deposit boxes, and he left me to privately go through my belongings.

When I opened the large metal box, a familiar black backpack greeted me. I checked inside to make sure that my spare ATM card and what few other items I'd brought to Seattle were still there. After thanking the manager, I went outside to the ATM and swiped my card. After entering my PIN and pressing the quick cash option, I input $100 for withdrawal.

An error message flashed on the screen: INSUFFICIENT FUNDS.

I tried again and got the same message.

I clicked back to the previous screen and selected the balance option. The ATM showed that my current balance was five dollars.

That was impossible. Days before I'd had just over a thousand dollars. If I had my dates correct, there should've been another deposit the night before from the government.

I marched back into the bank and found the same manager who'd helped me before. I explained the situation, and I asked if he could look into it for me. He was happy to help. After a couple minutes of scrolling through screens, he informed me that three withdrawals were made the night before, but no money had been deposited. He even looked to see if there were any pending deposits, but there were none.

I still had some cash stashed back at my apartment, so money wasn't really my concern. The manager canceled my stolen bank card and put a hold on my account.

"I don't know what to tell you about the deposit," he said. "Maybe you should contact the local VA."

I thanked him for his time and exited the building.

As I waited for Tanner to make his way across traffic, I thought about what could have happened. There was always the possibility that the government had screwed up. It was the government after all, and screwing up was its mission.

But the timing couldn't be a coincidence. Maybe Tanner would have some answers. Maybe he could leverage his position at the VA and help me find out what had happened.

"That took a while," Tanner said, as I got my seatbelt buckled.

I told him what had happened and asked him what he thought.

"It won't be difficult to figure out if there's an issue with the deposit. I can make a call to a friend in disbursement if you want."

"That would be great."

After a fifteen-minute call with his co-worker, Tanner hung up the phone. He was looking at me funny.

"What?" I asked. Nothing of what I'd overheard on his side of the conversation gave any indication of what his friend told him.

"Are you sure you didn't change your direct deposit information?"

"What do you mean?"

"My buddy at the VA says you submitted paperwork changing your direct deposits to another Seattle bank. The system made the change right before cutoff yesterday."

"I didn't change anything. Are you sure?"

"That's what my buddy said," Tanner answered.

"Could someone be messing with the system? I mean, it's possible that a VA employee did it, right?"

Tanner shrugged, but he didn't look convinced. I could see that he was wondering if I was the liar now. First his brother and now me.

Then I remembered what Rose had told me about her

son. His disability checks were still being deposited and supposedly he was still in Seattle. Could the two situations be connected?

"Can you call your friend back and ask him what bank the direct deposit's going to?" I asked.

"Sure, but I don't see—"

"Trust me."

Tanner didn't look like he did, but he picked up the phone anyway.

THIRTY MINUTES LATER, I was standing across the street from Rose's apartment building. From what I could see, there didn't seem to be any activity inside.

I told Tanner to stay on the street; I hustled across and entered the building behind an old man holding a pair of shopping bags.

The old man looked at me dubiously, but I was quick to say, "I'm visiting Rose on the top floor."

His visage softened and he said, "Give her my best, will you? Tell her Sanford says hello."

I held the door for Sanford, even offering to help carry his bags, but he shooed me away and I headed for the stairs.

Rose's door was locked when I tried the knob, and there weren't any signs of forced entry other than the old crowbar marks I'd seen the other day. I put my ear to the door and listened. Nothing. I waited. Still nothing.

My knocking produced no signs of life, so I grabbed the lock pick kit I'd been storing at the bank. I worked on the lock and twenty-three seconds later, I was in. I was rusty.

What concerned me was the door opening indicated the additional locks and chains were undone. I slipped inside and eased the door closed.

"Rose?" I said, taking in the room that looked like there

had never been a scuffle. Even the sink was clear and dishes sat waiting in the drying rack.

The first place I searched was the closet from where the two men had ambushed me. There was nothing there except for Rose's clothes and various storage boxes. I wasn't surprised that Rose was gone, so I tried to put her safety out of my head for the time being. There was something I needed to see first.

The stacks of letters were right where Rose had left them. I rifled through them, scanning each one for any clues of where her son might be. Nothing jumped out except for the dreary tone of Jonathan's musings.

I hit gold when I found the bank statements. It was the same bank that my government deposits were now going to, Pacific Bank & Trust. After jotting down the address on a piece of scrap paper, I glanced through the rest of Rose's collection of letters, but I found nothing else of use.

My cursory search of the apartment didn't turn up anything new, so I left the way I'd come, careful to lock the door on the way out. I checked to make sure everything was the way I'd found it.

Tanner was waiting where I'd left him.

"Was she there?" he asked.

"No. Do you know where this is?"

I handed over the address of the bank.

"Sure. It's about ten minutes from here, twenty with traffic."

"Okay, good. Let's go."

THE PACIFIC BANK & TRUST was tucked into a rundown strip mall on Mercer Island, just east of downtown Seattle.

"Let me see what I can find," I said when we pulled into one of many empty parking spots.

"I should come with you."

"Better you stay here."

I didn't want to get Tanner further involved than I had to. He'd already saved my life, and the last thing I wanted to do was get him in trouble with the law.

He didn't protest.

When I walked into the small bank, its sad door creaked with effort and then slammed behind me. At first, I didn't see anyone. There must have been some sort of an alert or chime, or maybe it was just the sound of the door, because a middle-aged woman with a soda in her hand came walking out to greet me.

"Can I help you?" she asked, sipping her soda.

"Yes, there's been some sort of mix-up at the VA, and I just learned my government deposits are coming to this bank."

Her eyes furrowed.

"That's strange, but I'm not sure there's anything we can do from this end. Have you tried the VA?"

"Yeah. They're working on the glitch, but they said I should probably come down here in case someone opened an account in my name."

The woman finished the soda and threw it underhanded it into a metal trashcan next to a desk.

"There's been a lot more of that than you'd think," she said, making her way to the computer, plopping herself heavily in the leather chair.

"Much more of what?"

"Identity theft. With the Internet, it seems there isn't much that people can't get their hands on."

"How about here? Have you had many cases at this branch?"

She didn't answer for a moment as she typed in her credentials. She looked up at me.

"I'm really not supposed to say."

"But you have had some?"

"Of course, we all have."

She looked like she wanted to say more, but instead she refocused on the screen.

"What did you say your name was?"

"Daniel Briggs."

"And did the VA happen to give you the account number where the deposits are going?"

"No, Ma'am."

"Can I see your driver's license?"

"Will an old military ID work?"

"You don't have a driver's license?"

"Stolen last night."

She looked up again, this time with a hint of suspicion, but when I handed her my military ID, she seemed to relax. Luckily I'd stored it in the safety deposit box or I'd be up shit creek.

"You were in the Marines?" she asked, handing the card back to me.

"I was."

She returned her attention to the computer and clacked away at the keyboard.

"My little cousin tried to get into the Marines. Says they didn't want him because of asthma."

I nodded, not really wanting to get into a conversation about someone who tried to get into the Corps.

"Ah, here it is." Her face moved closer to the screen. "That's strange."

"What's that?" I asked.

"Are you sure you didn't open this account?"

"I'm very sure."

"I say it's strange because the account was opened yesterday. Its identification number tells me that it was opened right here, in this branch."

I didn't like where this was going.

"How is that possible?"

Before she could answer, a male voice called from the back.

"Amy, do you want anything from KFC?"

"I'm okay," Amy called back, still clicking her mouse. "Hey Patrick, would you mind taking a look at something?"

A stubby guy with a thick head of toupee rounded the corner. When he saw me, his eyes immediately lit up.

"Mr. Briggs, isn't it?"

I had to grab onto Amy's desk to keep from stumbling backward.

"Do you know me?"

Patrick's smile widened.

"Of course. I helped you open an account yesterday."

Amy looked up at Patrick and then back to me. The suspicion was back.

"You say I was here yesterday?" I asked, incredulously.

"Unless you have a twin. I'm very good with faces and names. Comes from being in the banking business for twenty years."

He was still smiling, but I could see that was about to change if Amy had anything to say about it. I needed information so I played along even though my insides were twisting in confusion.

"Was I alone or was someone with me?"

Now Patrick's exuberance faded.

"You were here with your brother Sam."

I didn't have a brother.

Amy was slowly getting up from her chair. I knew that look. She was about to press the panic button and then all bets were off. I went with the most absurd story I could think of, hoping that I could play off their heartstrings.

I shook my head, doing my best to look downtrodden.

"I'm sorry; I just remembered. It must be this medication they've got me on. It causes forgetfulness."

Amy's alertness slipped a notch, and I could see the pity replacing it.

"Were you in the war, Mr. Briggs?" Patrick asked, his voice suddenly sweet, almost with a southern accent, using that patronizing voice I'd always hated from my mother.

"I was. That's why I'm on the meds," I said, hating that the words were coming out of my mouth. But at least Amy was calmer now, her finger off the emergency bell. "Just so I can remember, but the guy I was with yesterday, was he blonde like me?"

"No, he had brown hair and wore a camouflage hat. I couldn't believe he could hold that much tobacco in his mouth. You both tore out of the parking lot in that big truck of his."

My blood went cold, and I did my best to keep the look of dumb confusion on my face.

CHAPTER EIGHT

As I walked back out into the sunlight, I felt like I was having an out-of-body experience. How had Aaron Gray (because who else could so perfectly match Patrick's description?) taken me to the Pacific Bank & Trust, gotten me to open a bank account and change my direct deposit, all without me having a single memory of the events?

I stepped off the curb to get into Tanner's car when I heard the squealing of tires off to the right. I looked up and saw a blacked-out Chevy Tahoe tearing into the parking lot.

Tanner saw it too and already had the car running. I yanked the door open and jumped in, the car peeling out as I tried to slam the door shut. I almost got thrown out, but Tanner grabbed the back of my shirt using his right hand, while holding the car steady with his left hand. He aimed for the opposite end of the parking lot. It would've been a lot uglier if the parking lot was packed. Luckily, we got to the other exit without hitting anything or anyone.

I could see silhouettes in the Tahoe now, but the tint was too dark to pick out anything else. Then again, it was hard to miss the assault rifle now pointing out the passenger window and aimed in our general direction. The person wielding it was smart enough to hold their fire as the SUV hit a curb, narrowly missing a parked delivery truck.

As soon as Tanner got us righted, my door finally slamming shut, the familiar sound of gunfire erupted behind us, and the car's back window shattered from the shots.

Tanner seemed to know where he was going, so I just ducked my head and buckled my seat belt. We screamed around corners and the first time I looked back, I saw that we'd pulled away, at least out of accurate range.

"Shit," Tanner said, pointing to the road ahead.

There was a cop car parked on the side of the road, the policeman chatting with an old lady pushing a shopping cart full of, most likely, her possessions.

"What should I do?" Tanner asked, slowing down even as the police officer turned in our direction.

"Pull up next to him," I said, rolling down my window.

Tanner looked at me like I was crazy, but slid to the curb anyway.

The cop was one of those pot-bellied types, not much for running, but his hand was already resting on the pistol secured to his hip.

"Officer, that Tahoe is following us. It's full of armed men—"

The cop hushed me with a raised hand, squinting through his thick glasses at the SUV that was almost there. His eyes went wide, pistol slipping out of its holster, while grabbing for the radio on his shoulder.

He didn't stand a chance. I winced as the rounds hit him in the chest. I tried to grab him and pull him toward the car, but he was already falling away from me, his eyes bulging, face slack. I knew what death looked like, and by the way he slammed to the ground, the life already drifting away, I once again knew the quicksand of doubt sucking me under.

Tanner was screaming now, his foot slamming on the gas pedal and we leaped forward. I remember sitting up straight, not caring if a bullet slammed into the back of my head, even as the SUV crashed into the back of Tanner's car. I felt none of it, just the deep despair of regret, that I'd made the wrong decision again, a decision that cost a man his life.

Come to me, death. Come to me...

I DON'T REMEMBER the rest of the getaway, but sometime later I surfaced from my stupor. Tanner was still driving. He had his eyes glued to the road, going the same speed as the cars around us. He glanced over at me.

"You okay?"

"I think so."

"What happened back there?"

I shook my head, trying to remember, trying to put the broken pieces back together.

"I don't know," I lied, not wanting to admit what I already knew, that I was damaged goods, a broken being that shattered the lives of everyone around him. I couldn't remember ever feeling so hopeless.

"You don't look good."

Of course I didn't look good. I'd just gotten a man killed, an innocent cop.

"Snap out of it, man!"

My gaze wandered over to Tanner, who was white-knuckled and red faced.

"Just drop me off somewhere, okay?" I requested.

"No, not okay. We need to tell someone about this. We need to get the authorities involved."

"Who cares? Stop and let me out."

"Who cares?! What do you mean who cares? I don't know

what happened to you, but you're not the Marine I remember saving countless lives."

"That guy is dead," I answered bitterly, wanting to forget it all.

Tanner huffed.

"You need help, Daniel. You really do."

"The only help I need is for you to stop this car and let me out."

I didn't want to argue. I was past all that. I didn't care about him, his brother or even about Rose. It wasn't my job to help. Hell, who would want my help anyway?

"You're not right, you know that? I mean, who just suddenly snaps, especially after all that you've seen? Hell, it's like somebody took over your body!"

Tanner slammed his hand on the steering wheel then, shaking me from my thoughts. "Why didn't I think of that before?" he asked, slamming the wheel again.

"What?" I asked, not really caring.

He was smiling now.

"What if...?"

"What if what?"

"What if it's not you, but that something else is going on inside your head?"

I didn't think it was likely and told him so.

Tanner ignored my retort and clicked on his turn signal, soon making his way across the expressway. He was finally going to let me out. But when the exit came and went, and a dozen suitable stops passed behind us, I asked, "Where are we going?"

"I have a hunch. Trust me."

I debated opening the car door and hopping out, but in the end I just went along for the ride, really not caring either way.

I DON'T KNOW how much time lapsed until we pulled up to a
large sign that said *VA Puget Sound Health Care System*.

"What are we doing here?" I asked.

"I want someone to take a look at you."

"For what?"

"Don't worry about it."

I wasn't worried about it. I laid my head against the
window and watched the world go by as Tanner searched for
a parking spot.

"Is this where you work?" I asked.

"No, I work at the VA office in Tacoma."

I nodded and went back to my window gazing.

I FOLLOWED Tanner down the sterile hospital hallway, passing
the check-in desk, ignoring the annoyed look of the nurse on
duty. He seemed to know the way, and I was about to ask him
how when he ducked into an office. I followed and found
myself in a not entirely comfortable twelve by twelve space
cluttered with paper and books. There was a man, I
presumed a doctor by the white jacket he was wearing,
perched on the deep window sill, like a child. His nose was
literally in a book, and when Tanner coughed, the doctor
looked up through thick old-school glasses. They looked like
the kind you might be issued in boot camp.

"Hey, Doc," Tanner said.

"Hello, Tanner," the doctor replied, not bothering to
come down from his seat. "To what do I owe this pleasure?"
His voice was just shy of snooty. He sounded and acted like a
guy who'd grown up without any money, but then learned to
change his personality after he went to a good school. I
disliked the guy immediately.

"I need a favor," Tanner said, ignoring the annoyance on
the doctor's face.

"What is it *this* time?"

"I think my friend here's been drugged or something."

Now the book came down, and he looked at me like I was a rare bug or animal specimen.

"You have my attention," he said, coming closer, looking me up and down.

"He was given something," Tanner explained while I tried to stay in the room. My heart was beating faster now, the creepy doctor only making the thudding worse.

"In what form?"

"Intravenous."

The doctor, whose name I saw was Singleton, grabbed my arm and looked at the tiny red dot where the IV needle had gone in. My whole body tensed, and I almost grabbed him by the hair and slammed him into the desk. But then he patted my forearm and went to his desk.

"I assume he's a veteran if you've brought him here?"

"He is," Tanner answered. It all felt so surreal that they were having a conversation about my well-being as if I were not in the room. It was yet another out-of-body experience for me.

"Fill out these forms and I'll have some tests run," Dr. Singleton said, handing Tanner a stack of papers on a clipboard. Tanner didn't take it.

"I was hoping we could do this off the record."

Singleton's eyebrows rose. "And I assume you have a reason?"

Tanner nodded.

Something unspoken passed between the two men, and a tiny slice of my brain wondered what it was. That sliver of curiosity was quickly consumed by my urgent need to leave. Flight felt like the best option, so I turned for the door.

"Wait," Dr. Singleton said. "I'll do it."

I'm not sure why I stopped, but I did.

What followed was a brief physical examination after which Dr. Singleton took three vials of my blood. We waited in a little break area, where nurses and doctors shuttled in and out with only the occasional, *"Who the hell are they?"* looks flashed our way.

Tanner was watching me. I could see him out of the corner of my eye. I kept my attention glued on the television.

A few minutes later, Dr. Singleton returned and motioned for us to follow. We went back to his office, where he promptly shut and even locked the door.

"Where did you say he was given this IV?" Singleton asked.

"I didn't," Tanner replied, stone faced.

"And how long was he given this drug?"

"Probably less than a day."

His gaze shifted over to me, for the first time looking at me like I was a human being instead of a laboratory experiment. He even took on the look of concerned caregiver rather than the detached boredom of a career death dealer.

"You've been given benzodiazepine," he said, speaking slowly now.

"What is that?" I asked, sending a single shiver down my body.

"It's a drug, typically prescribed for chronic anxiety and for lack of sleep. You've heard of Xanax or Ambien?"

I nodded.

"Yes, well, you've been given a form of those popular drugs, and that in and of itself would not normally be a problem. These drugs, while considered safe by many in my profession, can lead to dependency among their users. This typically takes a period of time, and that is what makes your case so...special."

I didn't like the way he said "special," and I let him know

with a look. If he registered my warning, he didn't care. He resumed his explanation.

"While there is no way for me to test the exact type of benzodiazepine you've been given, much less the dosage, I can deduce by your withdrawal symptoms that it must have been a large dose, or perhaps a new generation of benzodiazepines altogether."

His eyes were lighting up now, like he'd just discovered a treasure map. I could almost hear the pieces in his brain clicking into place.

"Tell me, have you felt any sort of disorientation, malaise, short-term memory loss or thoughts of suicide?"

I didn't have to answer because the surprise in my eyes gave me away.

"I knew it," he said, clapping me on the arm.

The jolt wasn't nearly as jarring as the revelation that I'd been subjected to a drug I'd never heard of that was causing me to think and feel in ways that were unnatural. My mind still felt foggy. I felt ambivalent about things I normally felt were important. But, at least now the curtains were parting, and I urged my mind to work faster.

"So what can you do for him, Doc?" Tanner asked.

"I can prescribe a lower dose of a benzodiazepine, possibly Klonopin or something similar."

"No way," I said, backing away. "I don't want another drop of that stuff in my body."

Dr. Singleton's hand went up, urging me to calm down.

"I understand how you feel, but if I'm right about this—"

"How do you know you're right?" I asked, desperate now.

"I don't," he answered calmly, "But the type of drug and the dosage I give you will be a tiny fraction of what I'm thinking you were given before. It should help reduce any feelings of anxiety and, within the span of a few days, you should be weaned completely."

It appeared I didn't have a choice. As the fog continued to clear, one memory came back with stark clarity, like a streaking missile into my subconscious. I'd begged for my own death, willingly, and without the slightest hesitation. Even in my altered state, I knew that wasn't right.

I sighed and said, "Fine. Tell me what I need to do."

CHAPTER NINE

I'd never taken drugs in my life. Sure, I'd had my fair share of Motrin in the Corps, but who hadn't? And yeah, I'd just recently considered Jack Daniels one of my best friends, but nothing that so altered me that my personality, however jacked up I was, just disappeared like someone had reprogrammed my wiring.

As I sat in Dr. Singleton's office, waiting for the low dose substitute drugs to kick in, I realized something else. The Beast inside, the primordial within me, had also disappeared. I was used to seeing him there, like a waiting panther, always watching, ready to pounce when I purposely or accidentally unlatched its chain. Whatever was in those enhanced drugs had quieted the Beast, and it was with great relief that I finally heard it purring within me, finally awakening from its drug-induced slumber.

"How do you feel?" Tanner asked. He hadn't left my side.

"Better, I think." I wasn't really sure. I felt more energized, which seemed strange considering the drug Dr. Singleton had given me, but I still felt a steady calm. I could have taken a nap if I'd wanted.

It was another hour before the doctor said we could leave.

"Take it easy tonight, and get some rest," he ordered.

"I'll try. Thanks, Doc," I replied.

When we got to Tanner's bullet-riddled car, he filled me in on some information he'd heard from someone at the hospital.

"The cops are saying it was a gang drive-by. That police officer is dead, so they're really pumping the neighborhood to see if there were any witnesses."

I'd replayed the whole episode while waiting in the VA hospital. I had been given a bottle of pills and told to take two each day for a month. It was now time to get back on track, and the first order of business was to remove Tanner from the line of fire.

"I think you should go to the police," I said.

"What? Why?"

"You've got a life here, Tanner. The last thing you need is to get tangled up in my mess."

"Hey, man, this is my mess too, remember?"

"Just because your brother is part of this, doesn't mean you have to be. Trust me, there's only one way this is going, and it's not gonna be pretty," I said. "Besides, I work better alone."

He thought about that for a second, after which he replied, "I'm coming with you."

I thought he might say that, so I just nodded and told him to head to his apartment. I could ditch him later. He really didn't know what he was asking for.

WE DECIDED to wait until nightfall. It was a risk, especially considering Rose, but I didn't see any alternative. It would be suicide to rush into the warehouse without a clue of what we were dealing with, and besides, Aaron Gray and whoever he was working with must have known I was missing from what Tanner had taken to calling The Juicing Room. Leave it to a Marine to come up with a name like that.

As for me, other than the mild drug-induced calm, I was feeling increasingly more like myself. I smiled as The Beast growled low and throaty in the depths of my being, its limbs shaking loose, and the strength and savagery returning.

"What?" Tanner asked, noticing my smile as we put the finishing touches on our plan.

"Nothing. So like I was saying, I'll take point. Let me take a look around and then we'll go from there."

Tanner knew better than to offer an alternative plan. I was the point, always had been, and would never relinquish the role.

"Promise not to start anything until after we talk?"

"Sure," I said, not really meaning it. If anyone got in my way... The Beast growled again, hackles raised and bristling.

TANNER HAD this habit of leaving the news on whenever he was home. It was annoying, but at least I got him to mute the volume. He said we needed to monitor the news for any word on the shooters from earlier in the day. They'd released sketches shortly after the incident, and somehow we'd gotten away without any mention or description of Tanner's sedan. There was always the possibility that the police were withholding that information, but Tanner didn't think that was likely.

"They have a pretty open relationship with the media around here, especially since the new mayor ordered them to be as transparent as he wanted," he'd said.

I couldn't imagine being part of a police department that operated that way, but at least it might help us in this situation.

Both of us were dressed in muted dark clothing. It was the best Tanner had. No good going in wearing his old digi-cammies and face paint. This wasn't the woods of Camp Leje-une. It was better to go in dark, yet incognito. We'd have to take public transportation, just in case Tanner's car was on the police radar. Best to blend in.

I shoved the rest of a cold cut sandwich in my mouth and was about to turn off the television when I froze. There, surrounded by police, and being escorted out of a police station, was Rose with her familiar shuffle and downcast face.

I grabbed the television remote and turned up the volume.

Authorities at the local headquarters of Veterans Affairs believe this woman, Rose Francis, took advantage of her son's veteran status for monetary gain. Documents released by the VA detail a woman with serious mental deficiencies, who somehow forged her now-missing son's signature to continue receiving his disability checks. Ms. Francis is being held at an undisclosed psychiatric hospital until her trial date is set.

In the next hour, we will have VA representative—

I clicked off the television.

"Is that the woman you were helping?" Tanner asked.

"Yeah."

Some good my help did.

CHAPTER TEN

A light outside the expansive warehouse flickered as we watched. There hadn't been any movement since we arrived an hour before. I had to put Rose out of my mind for the time being. The only way I could help her now was to unravel the mystery and tackle the mastermind behind it.

The warehouse was situated in an industrial area of Ballard, just north of central Seattle. The air smelled of sea water and fish. I knew from previous visits to the area that a lot of fishing boats came in and out of Ballard, as they had for over a century. The residential section of Ballard had seen a recent resurgence, its old Dutch residences getting a welcome fresh coat of affluence. But from what I'd seen, the warehouses on the water hadn't changed, with each still sporting decades of rust and countless coats of pointless paint.

This warehouse was located within the industrial area. Solitary despite its proximity to its neighbors, the fencing looked strong and egress routes were clear where needed. There wasn't a single vehicle in the tight parking lot, and Tanner said it had been the same the night before.

"I think they keep their cars inside," he'd said.

It made sense. Who knew what elements prowled the warehouse district at night?

"I'm going in," I said.

"Don't do anything stupid," he said, smiling.

It was an old joke, announced by thousands of troops over the centuries.

I returned the smile.

"No promises."

We exchanged a quick nod, and I was on my way.

From shadow to shadow, I moved. No sign of surveillance or video cameras. I took my time to stop and listen. It was one thing to assault a target with a platoon or a squad at your back; it was quite another to go in alone.

So with nothing more than my lock pick kit and my hands, I crept closer. Still no sign of life.

By the time I got to the ladder leading up to the roof, I was one hundred percent sure there were no eyes on me. It was almost impossible for anyone except the world's elite snipers and special operations troops to be that quiet. Lucky for me.

I took the ladder two rungs at a time, careful to account for loose screws or rusted hinges that might give up my position. Up I went, slowly and animal-like. I was there again, in full warrior mode, my radar scanning as the rest of my body moved in clock-like precision. A single unit performing complex taskings led by the instincts of The Beast.

I stepped over the top rung, still scanning. There was nothing to register except for a slight breeze and the dinging of a buoy off in the distance.

It was twenty feet to the second floor window that would serve as my entrance. I counted off each step as I imagined Tanner watching me from the fence line.

The window was unlocked and cracked open. I peered

into the darkness, but my vision couldn't penetrate any farther than a couple meters.

Slow, I reminded myself, easing the window open, just waiting for it to squeal in protest. It didn't, and I was soon standing just inside, letting my eyes adjust to the gloom. I was in a carpeted office with a hulking desk in one corner. There were no chairs, no filing cabinets. It felt as abandoned as it looked.

It's easy to imagine all sorts of traps and snares when you go on alert into an urban environment. A total idiot could defend a building from assault with the right tools. A couple of grenades and some fishing line could, and has, wreaked havoc on warriors from Iraq to Malaysia.

While it's important to keep those very real threats in mind, when you've done it enough times, you get a feel for things. Dead corners. Fire lanes. Kill zones. But in the end, you have to press forward.

That's what I did in an exaggerated crouch, deeper into the gloom.

Soon I was in a short hallway with three identical offices lined in a row. After a cursory glance inside each one, I moved toward the stairs. I made it to the first floor without incident, and when I opened the door to what I correctly assumed was the main warehouse, the smell hit me, eliciting an instant response in my brain.

The memories washed over me like a ghost, blinding me for a moment. I remembered the deep sleep, the thoughts of drifting and of death. I hadn't noticed the smell at the time, but now I remembered.

The smell was like the peach air freshener they use in department store bathrooms. The sweet odor was strong, and then I recognized other smells, remembered from years on the battlefield. They were the smells of fear, the stale stench of human sweat, and many bodies in one place.

I shook off the memories and stepped inside the cavernous room, my feet planted wide, hands ready, and my body slightly tense for an oncoming attack.

Nothing.

No movement.

No lights.

No beds with people attached to IV bags.

Nothing.

The warehouse was empty.

AFTER A QUICK SEARCH of the building, I left the way I came in. Someone had done a speedy job of cleaning up things. Other than the air fresheners I'd found mounted at various points along the metal walls, there was nothing except some office furniture that had been too heavy to move.

Tanner was waiting, his look expectant.

"Empty," I said.

His eyes narrowed.

"What? How is that possible? The place was full."

I didn't know so I didn't offer an answer. Instead, I picked up my black backpack and headed back the way we'd come.

Tanner grabbed my arm.

"Hey, what do we do now?"

I looked down at his hand and he released his hold.

"We need to go."

"Where?"

"We need to go find your brother."

"Not before I found you," came the voice from behind. I whirled around to find Aaron Gray standing in the moonlight, a familiar shotgun in his hands. How had he snuck up on us? Either Tanner was the worst sentry in recent memory or I was losing my touch. Maybe both. "Looking for something?" Aaron asked, leveling the question, and the shotgun, at me.

"Where did you take them?" I asked.

"I don't know who you mean," he answered with a wicked grin. "And you, big brother, I'm surprised you're in on this."

"What the hell are you up to, Aaron?" Tanner asked, taking a step closer to his brother.

"That's far enough," Aaron said, swiveling the weapon on Tanner. He was too far away to rush. Even if we'd coordinated our attack, I was fairly sure that the younger Gray would take one, if not both of us, out.

Tanner stopped and looked over at me. I was Snake Eyes, after all, the guy everyone looked to for help. Why shouldn't Tanner do the same?

"What did you do to Rose?" I asked.

Aaron spit tobacco juice out the side of his mouth.

"You saw the news?"

I nodded.

"Then you know the answer. Little Miss Rose is responsible for taking advantage of her wounded warrior son. Now, I'm sure the authorities will be more than happy to find out that poor innocent Rose has also been in the middle of the same scheme involving a lot of other returning veterans. Sure, she'll spend a little time in a mental ward, but as soon as they piece together the whole thing, I know they'll figure that she's just as sane as you and me. I mean, a crazy person couldn't be the mastermind behind the theft of millions of federal dollars."

"You're insane," I said, with a touch of The Beast in my voice. It begged to be released, but I held it back. No use leaping to our deaths right now.

Aaron chuckled. "You might be right, but aren't we all a little crazy? I've read all about you, Daniel Briggs. Hell, you're right up there with Carlos Hathcock, for fuck's sake." He shook his head and I knew what was coming. "Up for the Medal of Honor and you can't even keep your shit together. Did you know that, big brother? Did you know that your hero here is just another PTSD pussy? Broken like the rest of those pathetic POGs (Persons Other than Grunts) in the Corps." His grin stretched from ear to ear, taunting me to action.

But then he surprised me completely.

"You're not worth my time, Briggs. Run back to whatever shit hole you came from. But this is the last time you get in my way, got that?"

He was letting me go? He must be insane, or maybe just delusional. Or maybe he did have such a stranglehold on things that we didn't have a chance. So far he'd had the uncanny ability to stay one step ahead, even sneaking up behind.

Staring down the barrel of his sawed-off shotgun, I didn't see any alternative.

"Fine. I'll go."

TANNER WAS quiet the whole way back to his place. What was left to say? We'd failed to find anything of substance, and his brother had somehow outmaneuvered us.

We said our subdued goodbyes outside his apartment. Tanner shook my hand and said, "Be careful out there."

"You too, and thanks for everything."

He'd saved my life. Not many people could claim that prize. It was usually the other way around.

Tanner nodded and headed inside. I waited on the dreary street, the Seattle sky yet again a blanket of mist. I left when I observed the light in Tanner's apartment click on. I debated staying around just to make sure he was okay, but decided against it. He was a big boy and it didn't seem that his brother would make a play.

So I left Tanner to his life, hoping that he'd get past what he'd seen. The last thing he needed was to get tangled into Aaron's mess.

As for me, I had other plans. No one fucked with me and got away with it.

CHAPTER ELEVEN

I walked the city until what I'd affectionately come to know as "The Glow" appeared on the horizon, rather than the real sun. The weather matched my mood, and I wiped away another coating of rain that had settled in my beard.

The city was waking now, shop owners unchaining doors and shooing the homeless from their doorsteps. As I watched a huddled form trudging toward Pike Place, I wondered how Rose was doing. She had to be scared and confused. Best case, I could do something to help. Worst case, she would be locked up for life.

It wasn't much to go on, and my options were limited by the meager resources I had available. It was just me and my backpack against Aaron Gray and a legion of forces that I hadn't even seen yet.

I regretted not doing more when I'd seen Aaron last, maybe offering myself as a swap for Rose, but every time that thought came up I pushed it away. I was no good behind bars. That would leave me no options.

So far Aaron had proved a worthy adversary, and I'd only

gotten a tiny glimpse of what was really behind door number two. He and his accomplices were somehow manipulating not only the VA system, but the local banking industry as well. It was possible that Aaron had patsies and informants within the VA, and if he did, that would make it much harder to upend.

I didn't want to admit it at first, but I finally realized that I needed help. After a quick search, I found a convenience store that had a pay phone out front. I slipped a couple quarters into the metal slot and dialed a number from memory.

"Hazard," came the familiar voice.

"Rex, it's Daniel."

Rex Hazard was an FBI agent who I'd served with in the Marine Corps. He was as good of a friend as I had. He'd helped me out a few months before in a little altercation I had in Boston, and I knew he tracked me when he could. That little fact annoyed me when he'd first told me, but I soon realized it was more out of brotherly concern than snooping.

"Holy fucking shit. Snake Eyes comes up for air once again!"

"I need your help, Rex."

His excitement dashed, he was all business. "Where are you?"

"Seattle."

I knew his number wasn't being traced; he'd promised me as much. It would still be a couple of years before the NSA had their talons clawed into the entire cellular network. Rex Hazard was in the business of recruiting and cultivating criminal contacts, so a secure line was a necessity. He was also savvy enough to not ask why I needed help or what I was up to.

"What do you need?"

I'd already thought it out, and rather than give him a list

of requests up front, I figured I'd begin with the only thing I knew was a definite lead.

"Can you get me the background on a guy named Aaron Gray? Did time in the Corps, not sure how long, but pretty sure he got out with a dishonorable."

"When do you need it?" Rex asked.

"Yesterday would be great."

Rex snorted. "The quiet one's always the smart ass. Okay, give me a few minutes. Can I call you back at this number?"

"Yeah, I'll be here."

I grabbed a coffee and a donut from the convenience store's limited menu and then settled in to wait. Traffic was picking up by the time Rex called back twenty-five minutes later.

"Well, you sure as shit know how to pick 'em," Rex said. "Aaron T. Gray, youngest son of Francine and Gilbert Gray. 0311 after boot camp and later selected to go to Recon. Record is clean, and he made it to Force with flying colors."

Not just anyone went to Force Recon. Back then there were no Marine Corps Special Forces. The elite, other than us snipers, of course, were Force Recon. Many of them would later get swallowed into what is now MARSOC (Marine Corps Forces Special Operations Command), and then predesignated MARSOC Raiders after the Raider battalions of WWII.

Rex went on. "Got in a couple fights, got demoted from sergeant to lance corporal. Looks like that's when the shit hit the fan. Lance Corporal Gray was drummed out of the Corps for running a drug ring out of his barracks room and master-minding the shipment of illegal arms from the Middle East. Says here he was convincing VIPs to take the weapons home in their luggage. All part of some fake campaign to help injured troops."

So, Aaron Gray was smart and cunning.

"Did he do any time in the brig?"

"Let me check." There was a pause on Rex's end, following by clicking and then he said, "Yeah, he was confined before and during his trial, did about thirty days after, but that's it."

"Is that normal?" I asked. I'd never heard of such a short sentence for those kinds of charges.

"I'm not an expert, but I seem to remember a lot of guys were coming back and getting into trouble. I wouldn't be surprised if some general quietly passed the word to flush the nonviolent ones out as fast as commanders could."

I had heard something about that. Troops returning from the battlefield often found "normal" life either too boring or a far cry from where they'd been. Getting drunk, picking fights and just plain trouble hounding were all things a well-motivated Marine could do with ease.

"Is there any information about where he went after getting out, like where he lives now?" I asked.

"His home of record is someplace called Yakima. I think it's north of Seattle. There's nothing else in the public record, or even in St. Louis, but a little digging through the FBI database found a Washington property with Mr. Gray listed as the owner. Looks like the shit kicker bought a place on Bainbridge Island. You know where that is?"

"Yeah. It's across the Sound from here."

I'd been to Bainbridge Island once after arriving. Bainbridge was a quick ferry ride away and scarcely populated compared to Seattle and its surrounding area. It was the last place I'd assume a disgraced Marine would live. Bainbridge Island was more a rich man's haven than a blue-collar hangout.

Rex must have sensed my spawning thoughts because he asked, "You're not planning on doing anything I wouldn't do, are you?"

That actually made me laugh. "You know me, Rex, always on the straight and narrow."

We both laughed at that, but I could hear the strain in his chuckles. He knew me better than most, yet I don't think even Rex had any idea what I was about to do.

CHAPTER TWELVE

The ferry ride to Bainbridge Island was uneventful. I was going the opposite way from most travelers. While the unloading at Seattle held a full house, the ride back across the Sound contained me, a host of what looked like night-shift workers, and a smattering of tourists. Everyone kept to themselves, some sipping Starbucks coffee, others napping.

I stayed on the deck, relishing the ocean air. That was one thing I never tired of: the ocean. I'd had my fair share of fights with the mighty behemoth in the past, but it never failed to calm me with its refreshing breath. I sucked in another lungful of cool air while the ferry's horn blasted and we made our final approach. I could see the line of cars from where I was standing, and for a moment I wondered if Aaron Gray was among them.

Not likely. At least that's what I told myself. I wanted a one-on-one encounter with Mr. Gray.

AARON GRAY'S home was a ten-minute walk from the ferry station. I passed by his mailbox, number 409, wearing a ball cap low over my eyes, always looking at the road ahead. There was plenty of cover in the tree line. When I felt like I'd gone far enough, I disappeared into the tree line. I doubled back, happy to find the way offered ample cover yet was easy to move through.

I was surprised to see that Aaron's house was a waterfront property. The structure itself was modest, all wood shingles and matching exterior, but the property did include a boathouse and a dock. There was no boat moored, so maybe Aaron used that to shuttle back and forth.

Waiting produced no movement from inside the house. There were no lights on that I could see, and the carport was empty. When I eventually moved closer I saw leaves covering the carport floor with no signs of recent passage. Besides, it didn't look large enough to house Aaron's massive truck. He must have a parking spot on the mainland.

It was easy to pick the locks and gain entry to the house. The interior provided even fewer clues as to Aaron's whereabouts. There was well-used furniture, but it all felt abandoned, like a summer home left during the winter.

Once again I wondered how he could afford a place like this. My simple upbringing couldn't fathom the price of such a house. I mean, the place had a view of downtown Seattle, and I sat staring at it from the massive bay window.

There were three bedrooms, all empty except for a single bed and a chest of drawers each in two of the bedrooms, and what looked like a queen bed with a small desk in the master bedroom. There were no clothes in the closets or the drawers. Even the bathrooms were empty, except for a sad roll of toilet paper in the half bath. If Aaron Gray owned the place, it had been a while since he'd been here. It was not what I'd hoped for. My thoughts of a confrontation withered as I completed my search of the home and moved to the boathouse.

There was an old canoe hanging off a wall mount with a hole in one side the size of a softball. It wasn't going anywhere soon. I did find a tackle box with 1950-era tools in it, but no clues.

I was about to make my way back to the ferry when I heard the sound of tires on gravel. When I looked up the drive, I saw a mail truck stop at Aaron's mailbox. The white-haired mailman deposited a stack of mail into the box. He then grabbed something from the floor and hoisted it out. It was one of those plastic boxes the post office uses to deliver mail that had been held for you while you were away.

I smiled at my fortunate break. With nothing left for me to do in Seattle, I settled in to wait. Someone was coming home soon, and I hoped with all my heart that it was Aaron Gray.

THE SHADOWS GREW long and I could feel the pine trees hugging in around me like a crowd inching closer to stay warm. Then the mosquitoes arrived, quiet and hungry. The only sign of their presence was the tiny welts and sudden itching along my neckline, then my hands and even my face. Their assault might have bothered me once, but that was a long time ago. I'd waded through too many swamps, slept in too many mud holes and braved too many jungle climes to really care.

The nuisance barely registered as I continued my vigil. Darkness fell and the shoreline was blanketed with the urgent calls of water fowl and the occasional splashes from fish leveling their own attack on the nighttime insects that inhabited the coastline.

The minutes clicked by and still I sat silent, waiting, hoping. And then a car stopped on the road, the driver exiting to pick up the mail. I couldn't make out the man's features specifically, but he had the general shape of Aaron Gray, even if I couldn't see the cheek full of chew.

The dark sedan coasted down the driveway, and the overhead lamp flickered on again as the driver exited. Now I saw the familiar scruffy face, the intense eyes of Aaron Gray. He gathered his mail and locked the car, apparently not at all concerned for his own safety. He didn't even look like he was armed.

I waited until he'd entered the house, lights flashing on as he moved from room to room. Ten minutes went by, followed by another ten.

I rose from my hiding place and went looking for the back door that I'd unlocked during my inspection of Aaron's home. It was finally time to pay him a visit.

CHAPTER THIRTEEN

I t wasn't hard getting upstairs. The house was sturdy and not a single step squeaked as I made the way closer to my prey. Most people think it's an easy thing to sneak up on someone. I'd found that was rarely the case. Usually there was something that told the target you were coming, like the scrape of a boot or the creak of old wood. Then there was the distance you had to cover. Being outside was one thing, but inside a building there were just too many angles, too many ways to be seen and ambushed. That's why only the best of the best took on the enemy in urban environments.

But this was one-on-one, and I had the element of surprise.

When I arrived at the top of the staircase the twang of some country love song floated down the hall. It was either coming from the living room or maybe from the kitchen.

I moved that way, silent and ready.

And then suddenly he was there, sitting at the kitchen table sifting through mail, his back to me. I gripped the box cutter I'd found in the boathouse. It would be quick and easy if things went south. But first I needed information, and I was willing to do anything I had to in order to get it.

Just as I went to take a step into the room, Aaron said, "Feel free to take a seat, Briggs."

I froze.

"I won't bite. I promise," Aaron said, still opening envelopes and tossing the junk mail into a pile.

The weapon in my hand dropped slightly. I didn't see his shotgun anywhere, and even though he could've had a weapon on his person, I was still confident that I could close the eight feet before he had time to react.

"Come on, man, have a seat."

For a moment, I thought I was experiencing side effects from my IV-induced sleep. I wondered if I was just imagining him speaking, because he sure as hell didn't seem to mind that I, a proven killer in wartime, was standing behind him.

"How did you know I was here?" I asked, still not moving.

"I talked to your buddy Rex Hazard. Man does that guy cuss like a corporal. He told me you were probably gonna pay me a visit."

What?

My stomach twisted. How did he know about Rex, and why in the world would Rex tell him I was coming?"

Aaron held up a phone. There was a familiar number on the screen.

"Call him if you want," he said, tossing the phone over his head without even looking.

I caught it and stared at the phone number. It was the same number I'd used to call Rex earlier that day.

My head spun and I grabbed the wall to steady myself. It took so much effort to remember whether I'd taken my medication when I was supposed to. Was I going down hallucination lane again?

Aaron was still working on his mail when I placed the call.

"Hazard."

"It's Daniel."

"You're with that Gray cat."

"Yeah."

"Look, I'm sure he's going to tell you the whole fucked-up story, so I won't waste your time. What I will tell you is that minutes after I talked to you today, I got a call from my boss who patched me through to multiple sources who will confirm Gray's story."

"What story?" I asked, confused and hurt Rex had gone behind my back.

"Just listen to him, okay?"

"Okay," I said, once again feeling like I had zero control of anything in my life.

I ended the call, walking the long way around the kitchen table. Aaron glanced up and asked, "We good?"

I slid the cell phone across the table. "No. We're not good."

He exhaled. "Give me five minutes. If you don't like what I have to say, you're free to leave."

There was something different about him now. He didn't have that same redneck brashness that had pissed me off on our previous encounters. He looked like the same guy on the outside, but something in his eyes and more refined tone were giving me a different vibe.

I didn't sit down, but I did say, "You've got five minutes."

"Rex says he told you about my time in the Corps, at least what he was supposed to see. My time in Recon and Force." His voice lowered as he continued. "Did you know Tanner in the Fleet?"

"No."

"But you were in the same battalion."

"Yeah."

His voice was flat now, void of all emotion. "I went into

the Marines because of him. I was there when he graduated from Parris Island. He was supposed to go to San Diego, but he put in a request to go to P.I., so I did the same, always wanting to be like my big brother. He's a couple years older, so it was natural, you know? By the time I joined him in Lejeune, he'd already been to Iraq and Afghanistan. I felt like I was way behind, but he didn't give me any grief about it. He'd picked up corporal by then and said he was on the short list to make meritorious sergeant. Then, when I was going through Recon Indoc, I got a call from Tanner saying that he was in a little trouble, and he needed me to come bail him out. When I got to the Jacksonville Police Department, they told me Tanner was being held on suspicion of drug and weapons trafficking. I gave them every penny I had, money I'd spent all of high school saving. Tanner paid me back later, but that was just the beginning.

"The cops didn't have enough evidence to make the charges stick, so Tanner never got in trouble with the Corps. He said it was just a mix-up, some deal he'd made with an old roommate that he shouldn't have. I was too busy to think about it much. You know how it is. Getting ready to get shot at takes you out of real world stuff."

I nodded. That was precisely why so many troops came back incapable of dealing with everyday life. Jam a needle of warrior ethos and battle readiness into an otherwise immature and insecure kid, and what do you expect him to do when he gets home? Some became adrenaline junkies and others ran to pills and booze.

"By the time I got back from my first combat tour, Tanner had changed. He'd picked up sergeant, but he didn't talk about the Corps in the same way he used to. He had that smooth-talking vibe of a barracks lawyer. You know what I mean. Anyway, I didn't like the guys he was hanging out with and told him so. He told me to mind my own business, and eventually we just drifted apart. With everything going on overseas, it was easy to put my head down and not worry about my brother."

He stopped and looked up at me. "Do you have any brothers?"

"Just my Marines."

Aaron laughed. "Yeah. Maybe that's what I needed. Fewer complications." He sat there for a few seconds, and then continued. "I'd just made it to MARSOC when my CO called me into his office. He said there was an NCIS agent looking for me. I met the guy at a McDonalds and he asked if I'd been in contact with my brother. I told him I hadn't. Then he asked me if I knew what Tanner was into. I told him I didn't. He didn't seem to believe me, but he pulled out a nondisclosure agreement and said that if I wanted to know what my brother was doing, I had to sign it. Like any good agent, he didn't make it sound like I had any other option. So I signed it, and he proceeded to tell me who Tanner had become."

Garth Brooks crooned from the kitchen as I waited for Aaron to continue. The younger Gray took off his ball cap and ran a hand through his matted hair.

"The guy said NCIS suspected that Tanner was the head of a group of Marines who were smuggling drugs and weapons in from the Middle East. They didn't yet know how it was being done, but they were pretty sure they had one of Tanner's buddies ready to testify. To make a long story short, the witness ended up killing himself in the barracks, and the investigation went nowhere. They were pressing Tanner hard then. Wiretaps, surveillance, really anything they could use. But in the end Tanner got off again. I never saw him during that time, I was usually off training or deployed, but NCIS kept me up to date. I think they were watching me too, and keeping me in the loop helped that effort.

"Tanner got out of the Corps and came back to Seattle. I

remember it to the day because it was the day I pinned on staff sergeant. Should've been one of the best days of my life. I was in MARSOC getting to be the warrior I'd always wanted to be. But Tanner's shadow showed up again, and this time he had an offer. NCIS said Tanner was taking his business to the civilian side, still using his government contacts. They needed someone who could get on the inside. Can you imagine, being asked to help take down your own brother? At first, I said no. It was Tanner's mess, and I didn't want to be part of it. But the NCIS agent was persistent, and he told me what he knew as he knew it. Tanner was targeting returning veterans. They didn't know how or why, but they knew it had something to do with the VA. It was right at the time when the VA was trying to get a better hold on PTSD and rising suicides.

"So instead of staying with MARSOC, I agreed to help NCIS. They drew up some bogus charges and even ran me through a real Courts Martial. The judge knew about it, of course, and even wished me luck after the trial, but my face was still splashed all over the *Marine Corps Times* and local papers. I spent some time in the brig and then got released. When I got back to Seattle, Tanner welcomed me with open arms, like I'd passed some kind of test. It was okay at first. We hung out and visited our mom up in Yakima. He even took me to a couple Mariners games. Everything looked good on the surface. He was in the process of searching for a new job, but he seemed to like living in Seattle. He had even hooked up with some people who helped homeless vets on the weekend. It was Tanner's idea to start the muffin truck."

Aaron let out a disgusted laugh. "He really knew what he was doing. I swear, if I didn't know what he'd done, and didn't have an idea of what he was still doing, he'd look like a really swell guy, someone the mayor gives the key to the city. It took a couple months, and then he introduced me to some guys he'd met at the VA. They were having a hard time getting meds for sleeping. Tanner suggested I help them find a way around the system, and he even arranged the meeting with a group that was not exactly on the up-and-up, but they claimed their only mission was to help wounded warriors. Man, short of flyers and business cards, these guys really seemed legit. They even had a counselor on staff who screened applicants, and even turned people away that were either considered hardcore addicts or needed to be committed to a mental facility.

"Tanner stayed hands-off, and I never saw him do a thing other than make introductions. He said he didn't want to get involved, that whatever I was doing was my business, and that his close call in the Corps had taught him a lesson. Some-times he'd ask me how things were going, and I would tell him, but other than that, he looked like another former Marine trying to find his way in the real world."

It felt a little rambling now, like a path snaking through the mountains that keeps circling back to the starting point.

"So what the hell does this have to do with me?" I asked, impatient for the punch line.

Aaron looked up as if he'd forgotten I was there and then recognition registered. He laughed.

"You? This *had* nothing to do with you. *You're* the one who stepped in the middle."

Blood rushed to my face and my hand clenched the box cutter.

"From the looks of your record it seems that you have one helluva habit of falling into deep shit."

"How did you know about me?" *If he says Rex, I'm gonna have to have a talk with my supposed friend.*

"You're kidding, right? NCIS has your entire file, except for the blacked-out stuff you did with the SEALs and MARSOC. Look, Briggs, I don't know how the hell you got here, and I don't really care. You're the one who was chasing me, remember?"

Had I really? That day at Pike Place felt like years ago. I almost couldn't remember where it had all started. Then it came back to me. Rose.

"What happened to Rose?"

Aaron nodded. "I took care of it, okay? She's in the safest place we could find."

"In a mental institution?"

He shrugged. "It was that, jail, or worse."

"What do you mean worse?" And then the image of the two guys at Rose's apartment popped into my head. I answered my own question. "Rose found out where her son went."

"Not exactly. The poor lady's been looking for a long time. Hell, I did what I could to help, in a roundabout way, but it looks like that kid may be long gone."

"But the money. Where's that going?"

"It's all part of the play. These guys are getting desperate vets to sign their money away."

I shook my head, still not understanding. "How? Why would they do that?"

A shadow passed over his face and he said softly, "Some guys will do anything to make the pain go away."

CHAPTER FOURTEEN

The pain. Did it ever really go away? I had to hope it did. The picture Aaron painted was dark and twisted, like Dante's Inferno.

He went on to explain his own growing role within the organization, and how he had to watch as former soldiers, Marines and some airmen were reeled in and ended up in what Tanner had called The Juice Room.

"They call them calming centers," Aaron said. "If anyone found out about them, all hell would break loose."

"Why don't they just kill them?" I asked. It seemed like the obvious way to prey on the wounded after they'd gotten what they needed.

"They haven't told me, but I have a couple guesses. First, I'm thinking they're keeping them around for insurance. Their fraud operation isn't fully functional yet, and I've already seen them wake a few guys up when more paperwork was needed for the VA. Second, and I can't be sure about this, but I think they're testing a new drug on them."

"How do you know?"

"I don't, but every few days new IV shipments come in and the labeling is a little different."

My mind raced back to the conversation with Tanner's doctor friend, Dr. Singleton. How could I have forgotten?

"Wait. Do you know about Tanner's buddy at the VA hospital?"

Aaron sat up a little straighter. "I haven't gotten any names, why?"

I told him about our visit, and about what Singleton had said about the benzodiazepine in my system, including his hypothesis that I'd been given a new version, something more potent.

"I wouldn't be surprised if this Dr. Singleton is part of Tanner's outfit," Aaron said. "What was your impression of the guy?"

I thought back, pushing past the murk I'd entered the hospital with.

"Smart guy. Not the best bedside manner. More bookish than clinical, I think." The guy was pretty nondescript, really. Like a co-worker you pass by every day for a year and can't recognize when you run into them at a bar.

Aaron thumped his knuckles on the table.

"This could be the 'in' we need."

"How?"

"Up until now, we haven't figured out who Tanner is working with. We get little sniffs, but that's all. I'll give my brother kudos; he knows how to stay under the radar."

I was still trying to put it all together. A Marine gone bad. A brother who left the Corps to bust him. A criminal organization that was essentially kidnapping military veterans and A) using them as guinea pigs, and B) taking all their money. What was next, zombies jumping out of manholes?

"What's the point of it all? I get that something needs to

be done, that they need to stop those people from being taken advantage of, but where's it all lead?" I asked.

Aaron pointed his finger at me. "Exactly. Where does it all lead? NCIS has its own theory, but I feel like something big is coming."

"Like what?"

"I don't know, but I have a sinking feeling that my brother's the one behind it."

————

TANNER GRAY SHUT his laptop and leaned back onto the couch, eyes closed. He'd come so far. From underpaid Marine to criminal mastermind. He understood how it might look to some, including his mother, but he'd found himself in that first simple transaction. A mechanic who was working on his HUMVEE in Afghanistan had mentioned in passing a nearby poppy plantation. When Tanner pressed him on it, the mechanic, who'd been busted down to PFC twice in his three-year career, shut his mouth.

Sgt. Gray had waited two nights to pay the Marine a visit. When he did, threatening to go to command with the charges if he didn't fess up, the PFC spilled the plan. He'd come into possession of three bags of heroin and was planning on shipping them back to his girlfriend in Arizona. He even admitted to repeated shipments earlier in their deployment. To Tanner's surprise, the Marine had never been caught.

Tanner had convinced the Marine to relinquish the drugs, which were vacuum-sealed and waiting in a manila envelope addressed to the girlfriend. In exchange, and as long as the Marine kept in line, Tanner promised not to turn him in. When the Marine asked Tanner what he was going to do with the drugs, Tanner said he was going to throw them in the burn buckets.

He'd left the relieved Marine and spent the night thinking about the package of drugs now stashed in his foot locker. Never in his life had Tanner considered getting into the drug business. But life in the Corps was getting old. He'd signed up thinking he'd become some kind of hero, like the guys he saw in the recruiting videos. Hook, line, and sinker was how he'd gone off to boot camp. Now things were different. He was a sergeant and he had some autonomy among the rest of the enlisted men of the battalion. The Staff NCOs and officers didn't bother him because they knew him as a reliable and squeaky-clean Marine. And up to that time he had been.

As he lay in his cot that night, dreaming of life back home, he started to wonder if his time in the Corps would be better spent in different pursuits. He decided to sleep on it.

When he woke up the next morning, his mind was made up. His first stop was the international phone booth, where there was already a line to call home. Too anxious to wait, he pulled rank in front of a group of lance corporals, promising to keep the call short.

That first call went to an old friend who was still living in Yakima, Washington. He told his buddy to expect a package, but that he shouldn't open it, that it was a present for his mom. The guy was cool about it and promised to keep it until Tanner's return.

After getting back to the States, Tanner took a couple of days leave and visited his mother. Before he went to her house, he stopped at his buddy's home with a bottle of Jim Beam in tow as a little "Thank You" gift. After a couple minutes of catching up, he left with the familiar manila envelope, shocked that it was still intact. He didn't have a clue what to do with the heroin, but he was sure he could figure it out.

So during his leave, when he wasn't catching up with old friends, Tanner networked until he got a bite. A low-level drug dealer who supplied the local high school with marijuana said he could see what he could get for the drugs. He only asked for a tiny sample, and he said it would take him a couple days to get it in the right hands.

The burnout called Tanner two hours later, asking if they could grab lunch at the Olive Garden. When the guy showed, Tanner saw him shaking. Tanner recognized that as excitement the guy was trying to hide. For his part, Tanner played along, acting stupid about the entire transaction. It took the dealer all of five minutes to slide a folded newspaper across the table and say, "That's five thousand."

Tanner shrugged like he was just happy to get it out of his hands, but in his head the possibilities blossomed from seeds to saplings. If the dealer was willing to give him five thousand dollars, that meant he was getting a bigger cut, and then whoever was even further up the line was doing the same thing. He left the Olive Garden pleasantly surprised to have five thousand dollars in his pocket. One thousand of the proceeds would go to his mother, but he was ecstatic about the bigger picture.

A little online research produced staggering numbers. The amount he'd been given was but a drop compared to the ocean of money the drugs could eventually go for on the streets. Like any good entrepreneur, he came up with a plan.

There'd been stops and starts during those first few months, and more than one of his accomplices had been nabbed by authorities, but there had always been a plentiful supply of disgruntled logistics sergeants, admin clerks and supply chiefs who wanted to walk away from the Corps with a bit more than the meager retirement they might one day make. Tanner always kept things cordial, and simply acted as the supposed middle man, only making introductions to key players who'd already been given the gameplay. The number one rule was DON'T GET CAUGHT.

It became an intricate web that Tanner ran from his barracks room and the base library. No one knew he was behind it all, and that made it all worth it. The money was great, to be sure, but the intrigue and gamesmanship was even better. Early on, he came to prize his anonymity, and happily paid others more in order for them to take the more visible roles. He never handled the drugs, and money drops were conducted far from Camp Lejeune.

As his network grew, the system became increasingly unwieldy. Throw in training and deployments, and mistakes were bound to happen. His first scare came, not from his drug business, but instead from a shipment of weapons meant for the streets of Chicago and Los Angeles. Tanner knew it would one day happen, but someone talked too much, and someone with the Camp Lejeune military police put part of the puzzle together. They never suspected his true role in the beginning, and only questioned him about the introductions he'd been privy to, but it was enough.

The fear never went away. What changed was his need for more. More sources. More intermediaries. And most importantly, more risk. The risk added to the reward. He dreamed about it. He tasted it with his morning meal and lapped it up like a lion drinking a gazelle's blood.

Soon he realized that his time in the Corps was coming to an end. He knew he was being watched, and it became increasingly difficult to do business while maintaining his role within an infantry battalion. He put in his papers, and after a lengthy fight with base admin (he suspected that NCIS had their hand in the delay) about some insignificant detail in his separation papers, Tanner took a final look at the Camp Lejeune main gate and drove to the New Bern airport.

When he returned to Washington state, the first thing he

did was blend in. He applied for odd jobs and looked for volunteer opportunities. Tanner was accustomed to military personnel and the strict hierarchy within the Marine Corps, so he rightly assumed that finding fellow veterans was the way to go. Most were only too eager to talk about the old days, and many didn't have a clue how to make a dime in the real world. They'd shuffle from job to job, always complaining about the lack of work ethic in the civilian world, or the fact that no one understood them. It was a perfect pond for Tanner to fish in.

He bonded with outcasts and well-transitioned former military alike. If his past experiences had taught him anything, it was that everyone needed a friend, and everyone hit hard times at some point in their lives. Relationships were cultivated as he shored up his contacts back east. He'd been careful with his money, and he had enough to sustain him for ten years. Tanner's patience was rewarded.

Within three short months, he had five candidates for the single position he was going to create. That person would be the face of the organization. He would be well compensated for the risk, which Tanner would minimize by only going through military channels for supply, thus augmenting, instead of competing, with the big-time drug traders in the area. This was a new funnel that Tanner hoped would eventually spread to the entire Northwest.

With his "head" in place, the initial and subsequent training would all be done remotely, without any knowledge that Tanner was behind it, and Tanner's man began his own recruiting campaign. Every candidate was routed up the chain, and Tanner used background checks and even private investigators to vet each one.

They had to be clean, with no more than a misdemeanor on their record. They also couldn't have any history of drug abuse. They would be monitored by random drug tests, just

like the ones they'd endured in the military. Pecker checker
and everything. In fact, much of what Tanner's budding organization became was modeled from the disciplinary structure
of the Marine Corps.

Every man was counseled by his superior. They were even
given housing allowances, instructed to wear appropriate
civilian attire, and encouraged to participate in activities that
gave back to the community. There were a handful of misfits
along the way, but they were dealt with swiftly, and warned
never to speak a word of their involvement for fear of
retribution.

But what made Tanner's organization truly special, what
separated it from the thugs and pimps on the streets, was
that the former Marine found a specific audience for his
products, and an industry willing to see it grow. The wars in
Iraq and Afghanistan had produced a new reliance on mood-
altering medications. America had already been on its way to
a new dependence on drugs like Ambien and Xanax, but it
was the introduction of returning troops that truly made it
more socially acceptable to use them. Doctors prescribed
Ambien like a baker doled out cookies. It was the new norm,
and the drug industry was salivating.

It wasn't just multibillion dollar corporations who were
looking at an increasingly drug-dependent populace. For
years, international drug lords had ratcheted up the flow of
illegal drugs to fulfill the insatiable appetite of Los Ameri-
canos. And Tanner Gray had read about it all. Like a PhD
candidate researching a groundbreaking expose, he'd put the
pieces together and leveraged his own experience to come up
with one startling conclusion. What if he could beat them
both by becoming the glue that took advantage of both the
legal and illegal drug worlds?

Tanner grinned as he let the familiar picture sink in, his
thoughts riding the waves of possibilities.

CHAPTER FIFTEEN

W e spent the rest of the night sifting through options. I was in favor of a full-on attack. We knew where Tanner lived, and it wasn't like he was hiding. It could've been as easy as me slipping into his apartment and taking care of things.

But Aaron was adamant.

"This is much bigger than Tanner. Think of the guys that are getting used. We need to help them."

In my experience, it was better to go after the snake's head. Without Tanner, maybe things would just sort of trickle out. Besides, despite being on the case for over a year, Aaron didn't have a clear picture of how Tanner was involved. It could all be a red herring and I told him so.

Aaron shook his head emphatically. "No. This is way bigger than even NCIS thinks. He's my brother, okay? I just have this feeling that he's prepping something huge, something epic."

I didn't know Tanner, and I doubted that Aaron really knew him either, but I didn't have the energy to disagree.

Without a clearly defined goal, my energy was on sub-level three.

"I need to get some sleep," I said. "Mind if I take one of the extra bedrooms?"

"Sure. Let me shake the dust off."

I waved his offer away. "I'm good, thanks."

At the time, I really didn't think the meds were once again sending me mixed signals, commanding me to sleep when really I should've been plotting with Aaron. By the time I got to the first guest room, my body was on autopilot. My eyes locked onto the bed and that's where I went, zombie-like, all thoughts of Tanner gone from my mind. The only thing I could think of was sleep – sweet, sweet sleep.

IT WAS inky black when I snapped awake. The quiet felt more like a heavy weight than a soothing calm. My heart was racing and I didn't know why. Another withdrawal symptom?

Then it hit me, the drugs Dr. Singleton had given me. Were they something other than what he'd told me? If he was in league with Tanner, the whole lecture about withdrawal could have been bullshit. I'd been too surprised by Aaron's revelations hours before to even think about it. The pills were still in my pocket and I yanked them out, disgusted that my head still wasn't firing on all cylinders.

Back and forth my mood and worry swayed. What the hell was wrong with me?

I threw the orange pill bottle across the room and it cracked against the wall, the lid still securely attached when it fell to the floor. It seemed like a metaphor for the safe I'd been trying to crack since meeting Rose. No matter what, the mystery box would not open and spill its secrets. Tanner had things buttoned up tight; it would take a lucky break to get any closer to the bottom of things.

I sat up in bed and closed my eyes. I'd never meditated before, and didn't really know what I was doing, but I tried it anyway: willing my mind to settle, ordering my once sharp intellect to get in line. I imagined lying on the ground again, my eye resting just behind my rifle scope. I'd spent countless hours that way, watching and waiting, centered on the task at hand. My breathing settled, coaxing my heartbeat back to a steady rhythm. In my head the image of a slowly swaying crosshair coalesced, and I took comfort in the familiar image, a thin smile spreading.

At some time later, my eyes eased open, the same image I'd been focused on still imprinted on my subconscious. I didn't care what Aaron said. I had one target in mind: Tanner Gray.

AARON DIDN'T TAKE the news well. He'd been up all night planning, but his plan was too passive for my tastes.

"All I need to do is get my hands on your brother," I said.

"I thought we talked about this. We need more evidence, more time."

"Tanner will give us anything we need. I'll beat it out of him if I need to."

This was way beyond helping an old lady find her son. Tanner had manipulated me, and if things hadn't gone the way they had with Aaron, who knew where I'd be? Probably hooked up to an IV again or drooling in a loony bin. It was personal now.

"What about the rest of them?" Aaron asked. "What about the people who are taking advantage of troops that raised their right hands just like you and me?"

I didn't want to think about them. It was all I could do to keep my mind focused on one thing. But I understood Aaron's concern.

"Look, if I can help, I will, I promise."

That seemed to settle him for the moment and we left without saying another word.

AARON HAD to check in with his criminal cohorts, so I took a bus from the ferry back into downtown Seattle. The streets were clogged with workers headed to whatever assigned cubicle they'd be chained to for the next eight hours. Not one of them gave me a sideways glance; I flowed in and out of their streams, careful to stay concealed from anyone who might be following me.

By the time I got to Tanner's apartment, I was sure I wasn't being followed. It was an outside chance, but I needed to be sure. I ducked inside the apartment building and made my way to Tanner's place. I passed it once, making my way farther into the complex.

I made a loop around the roughly circular set of buildings, and returned to Tanner's door. There was really no easy way to do it, so I settled on knocking. No answer. I was about to pull the lock pick out of my pocket when I heard footsteps coming down the hall. It was just a couple of girls in workout tights and tanks chatting away as they sipped from oversized Starbucks cups.

I stared at the door like I was waiting for someone to answer, and nodded at them when they passed. One of them gave me a smile and giggled, eliciting an eye roll from her friend.

"You and blonde guys," the eye-roller said.

I smiled, waited for them to turn the corner, and then set about picking the lock.

The apartment was just like I remembered it, only this time no Tanner. I was just about to start looking around when I heard footsteps from the hall. I froze and waited for them to pass. They stopped at Tanner's door. Nothing happened for a few seconds, and then I heard the jangle of keys.

I slid into the bathroom and hid behind the door. It offered me a perfect view of the entrance.

The lock clicked and the doorknob turned. It wasn't Tanner who entered, but a chubby guy with a blue uniform and an armful of paper bags. He set one on the kitchen counter, shifted the rest of the bags in his arms, and then exited the way he'd come, locking the door on the way out.

I eased my way back into the main living area and peeked in the bag. It was laundry, neatly folded and ready for wear.

After a fruitless search of the apartment, I weighed my options. I could lay in wait. That was the obvious thing to do, but I ached to do anything but wait. Tanner was the key to the whole operation, but maybe there was someone else who could get me a look inside.

LESS THAN AN HOUR LATER, I was standing outside the same VA hospital I'd visited with Tanner. The parking lot was full and the waiting room packed as I made my way past men in wheelchairs and little groups swapping war stories. The patients were spread among eras from World War II to the current battles in the Middle East.

No one seemed to be in any rush, and the whole room had more the feel of a VFW than a hospital waiting room. I wondered if this was how they spent their days. I imagined myself in a wheelchair, propped in a corner, letting the years drift by. I shivered at the thought, and Aaron's words, no matter if they were for his brother's benefit, echoed in my mind. *You're broken. You're broken.*

Shaking off the vibe, I passed the same annoyed nurse from the day before and headed toward Dr. Singleton's office.

He was talking with a colleague when I got there, and I knocked on the door jamb to get his attention. Singleton glanced in my direction, and he said, "Ah, it's you again. Will you excuse me, Glen?"

The other doctor left, and I entered the office.

"What can I do for you today, Mr. Briggs?"

"I need to know what you gave me."

He ignored my question.

"Feeling better?"

"Not exactly," I said.

"Don't forget that I did tell you about possible side effects. They may linger for some time."

"Cut the crap, Doc. What did you actually give me?"

He seemed genuinely surprised.

"A very low dose of Klonopin, like I explained on your last visit." And then he cocked his head. "What are your symptoms?"

I didn't want to play along. It had to be what he'd given me. It was the only explanation that made sense. The only alternative was that I really was messed up, and that maybe whatever was in the IV triggered sort of a chain reaction.

Maybe it was the way he looked at me, like he was genuinely curious, that made me answer.

"Some paranoia," I said, unsure of how much I should admit.

"Heart palpitations?"

I nodded.

He stared at me for what seemed like an eternity and then mumbled, more to himself than to me, "Then it's more complicated than we thought."

"What's more complicated than you thought?" I asked, watching as he seemed to fall farther inward.

He didn't reply, just stood there staring.

"Doc, what is it?"

His quiet contemplation was starting to piss me off. I felt the edges of a coming storm blowing in over my mental horizon.

It wasn't me but the intercom on the wall that finally got his attention.

"Dr. Singleton, you're needed in room two nineteen," said a female voice.

Singleton walked over to the intercom, pressed the button and said, "I'll be right there." He turned to me and said, "I'm not sure how long I'll be. How can I reach you?"

"I can wait," I said, when what I really wanted to do was shut the door and shake the answers out of him. As if the universe had just read my thoughts, a security guard passed by the open doorway.

Singleton pursed his lips, and then said, "Very well." He turned and was gone, leaving me to wait once again.

The first couple of minutes I just roamed around his office, taking in the medical school diploma from LSU and the PhD from Stanford. Papers and dog-eared books littered every flat surface including the only other chair in the room. The place was a real mess. How the hell did he find anything in the clutter?

There was a picture of Dr. Singleton in a lab coat holding up a clear container filled with blue pills. He was grinning from ear to ear. When I looked closer I realized he was in some kind of factory. That made me go back to the diplomas on the wall. The PhD from Stanford said *Biomedical Engineering* in bold. I went to the medical school diploma; that one said Dr. Singleton was an Internal Medicine physician.

What was a normal Internal Medicine doctor doing with a Biomedical Engineering degree? My eyes went from the diplomas to the picture of Singleton holding the plastic container full of pills. Something wasn't right. What did Tanner Gray have to do with Singleton?

That got me sifting through the books and papers. There were reports that I didn't understand stacked on top of hand-written notes. Books on FDA drug trials mingled with *Fortune* and *Inc.* magazines.

I felt the familiar tingle in my hands, like I was onto something and it was so close, maybe even within reach. The puzzle had me so consumed that I didn't even notice when Dr. Singleton came back.

"What are you doing?" he asked.

I didn't care that he'd found me snooping through his things.

"Just doing some light reading, Doc," I said, continuing my search.

That's when he made his first mistake. Singleton grabbed my arm and tried to pull me away from his desk. No sooner had he touched me than I spun and grabbed the front of his shirt with one hand. His eyes went wide.

"I'm sorry, I—"

I grabbed the door with my free hand and slammed it shut. Dr. Singleton tried to move but I had him held fast.

"Tell me what you and Tanner are up to, now." The words came out of my mouth laced with venom, leaving no room for interpretation or discussion.

He gulped twice and glanced at the door, or maybe it was the intercom. In response I slapped him hard. He would've crumbled to the floor if I hadn't pinned him against the wall.

"I don't know what you mean," he said, his voice coming out in whimper.

"How do you know Tanner Gray?"

"We...we met at a VA networking event, I think."

I slapped him again.

"Don't think," I said.

He was shaking now, a man unused to physical violence.

"He found me."

"Why?"

He looked toward the door again, and just as I was about to slap him, there was a double knock, all authoritative.

"Dr. Singleton?"

It was a male voice.

"Tell him you're busy," I whispered.

He looked like he was going to ignore my order, but he finally got his quivering lips under control enough to say, "I'm busy."

"Sir, you said it was urgent."

Singleton's eyes bulged further and the fear marring his face told me all I needed to know. He'd requested security when he'd left the office. They were there for me.

"Tell him you made a mistake," I said.

Singleton nodded, but then, with the last strength he probably had left in his body, he yelled, "Help me!"

This time my punch knocked him senseless as I lunged for the door, the knob twisting and the door opening in sudden slow motion. I barreled into the door with my shoulder and latched the lock. There were shouts in the hallway and I looked for some way to escape. The only way was the window, which looked old and sturdy, like a World War II relic. There was no way to open the window, probably because the office was on the first level, so I did the next best thing.

I grabbed the office chair, hoisted it in the air and flung it at the window. It bounced off, but I saw a hairline fracture there. I picked the chair up, and gripped it as well as I could and bashed it again and again, even as I heard similar noises coming from the office door.

Finally, and with considerable effort, the thick window was cracked enough that I was able to jump up and grab the metal frame and swing outward, my feet finishing what the chair had started. The entire pane of shattered glass fell to the mulched ground as I followed it right into a prickly decorative tree.

I glanced over my shoulder to see three security guards entering the office, one man pointing at me. It was too late for them. I was already running, and when I wanted to disappear, there wasn't much a couple of rent-a-cops could do to stop me.

CHAPTER SIXTEEN

The bravest of the three security guards went for the broken window and only then pulled his holstered pistol. It shook a bit in his hands, and other than his limited time at the range, he'd never had a chance to fire it.

"Let him go," said Dr. Singleton, from where he sat on the ground, rubbing the welt on his cheekbone.

The lead security guard hazarded a look outside, as if he were going to follow the escaped lunatic, but he hesitated.

"We should call the police," he said.

One of his companions looked like he was going to say something, but the fact that he was severely overweight and in no condition to outrun anyone, made him hold his tongue. He nodded instead.

"No," said Dr. Singleton, who was now getting up with the help of the third guard, a skinny kid who looked more like a middle school student than an adult. "Please let him go."

The lead guard made another move like he was going for the window, but it was only for show. He did keep his weapon in hand when he said, "We'll need to file a report for the hospital." By the look on the man's face, it was obvious that such an act would be an inconvenience.

"I'll take care of it," Singleton said. "He is my patient, and I'll be happy to explain the circumstances to whoever I need to."

"Well, okay. I'll have the new kid write it up," he pointed at the skinny guard, "and then he'll need to get your signature."

Dr. Singleton nodded and started shooing the men from his office.

"You should get that looked at, Doctor," the senior guard said, motioning to Singleton's face. "Could be broken."

Dr. Singleton opened and shut his mouth a couple of times to prove there was no permanent damage; then ushered the men away.

He closed the door as soon as they'd left, and stared at the broken window. Tanner had said the Briggs character was gone, so he'd been surprised to see him show up unannounced. Then again, the adventurous side of him that took flying lessons from a retired fighter pilot relished the idea that a wild man was on the loose. It made it all so much more fun. He'd never served in the military, but he was surrounded by veterans, and many liked to tell their stories. He listened quietly, always absorbing the best tidbits, and filing them away for some future date when he might pen a memoir.

His cheek throbbed, but he had access to any number of drugs that would make the pain go away. He wasn't in the habit of taking the pills he so often prescribed. It was one of the things he prided himself on: He could reside in a world of swirling possibilities, and he never felt tempted--not even when surrounded by cocktails that could make a sane man crazy, a crazy man whole, or by drugs that could make you feel like the king of the world.

No, he'd rather be one of the architects behind it all,

researching and fabricating until the inevitable stroke of fame hit.

But none of that would happen if this Briggs character got the word out. Singleton picked up his cell phone and placed a call. Tanner Gray answered a moment later.

"Tanner, your friend Daniel Briggs just paid me a visit, and I don't think he'll go away quietly."

———

TANNER PLACED the cell phone on his desk and looked around his cramped cubicle. His new job at the VA required a normal nine-to-five workday, and although most days he completed his work in three hours, he was still expected to stay until the proverbial bell rang.

At the moment, he didn't care about dropping the job to take care of his real business. To hear that Daniel had returned wasn't really a surprise. The guy was messed up. Top that with the experimental meds he'd been given as well as whatever mixture Dr. Singleton had prescribed, and Tanner was sure the former sniper was walking a thin line of sanity.

He wasn't worried about Daniel finding out anything. Tanner was always careful and cautiously paranoid. Not a shred of evidence would ever be found in his apartment or on any of his personal computers. With the Internet, he could communicate with those he needed behind the safety of absolute anonymity. No one, not even the NSA could tie him back to any illegal activities. Tanner knew how to play the game, and he played it very well.

But, the timing of Daniel's reappearance could not have been worse. His carefully laid plans were coming together; a wrinkle like Snake Eyes was the last thing he needed. Maybe Aaron would have an idea of where the sniper was. His brother had turned out to be adept in not only infiltrating the enemy drug camp, but he'd somehow kept tabs on Briggs. Whatever he'd learned in the Corps was definitely paying off, and Tanner needed those skills on his side. Maybe it was time to bring him in all the way.

He called his brother from the office phone and suggested they grab lunch.

"I'm pretty busy," Aaron said. Tanner could hear loud machinery in the background and it was nearly impossible to understand his brother.

"We need to talk about an old friend," Tanner said, hoping his brother would pick up on the reference.

"Who?"

"The guy that was with me the other night."

More grinding and whirring on the other end and then Aaron said, "Okay. Meet me at our usual spot in an hour."

———

THE SANDWICH SHOP was across the street from a rundown auto repair shop that looked like it might cave in on itself at any minute. The building housing the eatery wasn't much better, but it did serve the best Italian sub Aaron Gray had ever eaten.

He'd gone ahead and ordered one for Tanner too, and didn't bother waiting, devouring the sandwich despite his concerns. Things were more than their typical busy day at "work," and the fact that Daniel was somewhere out there had kept Aaron on edge all morning. Then, to get the phone call from Tanner only made things worse. The guy running the show at the warehouse told him not to go, but Aaron made a real show, and the guy finally relented. The entire way to the lunch spot Aaron ran through possible scenarios, but with no way of contacting Daniel, they were all shots in the dark.

Tanner showed up just as Aaron was finishing the first half of his sub, and he tried to play it cool by merely giving his older brother a nod, while tearing into the second half.

"Thanks for waiting," Tanner said wryly.

Aaron just kept eating.

"How are things?" Tanner asked, unwrapping the sub from its oil-stained paper cocoon.

"Busy," Aaron said through a mouthful of food.

"I might need your help."

Aaron looked up. It was the first time his brother had admitted to needing anything, except for the time he'd needed bail money in North Carolina.

"What do you need?"

Tanner took a bite of his sandwich and looked out the window.

"I need Briggs to disappear."

"I thought he already had," Aaron said, drinking his soda.

"He was supposed to be gone, but he just showed up again."

Aaron snorted, playing the smart ass he'd perfected during the previous year. "Sounds like your problem, not mine."

Tanner set down his sandwich and glared at his brother. "Look, I know I've never let you in on this, but it's important."

"Let me in on *what?*" Aaron asked, the tingling in his ears matching the butterflies in his stomach.

"I've got something big going, okay?"

Aaron laughed. "You mean your big job at the VA? Give me a break."

Tanner shook his head. "No, it's something else."

"You'll have to do better than that, big brother. You ask me to make someone disappear, and you don't even tell me why?"

He'd never seen his brother so flustered. Aaron wondered what Daniel had done.

"You make it sound like I want you to have him killed," Tanner said.

"Isn't that what you meant?"

"No, dammit. I only meant that, well, maybe you should put him back with the others."

So Tanner wasn't a murderer, but he had no qualms about ruining someone's life. Aaron figured he had his brother right where he wanted him.

"So what's this big thing? You gonna win the Lotto?"

Neither Aaron nor his NCIS handlers knew what the elder Gray's true goal was. They assumed it had to do with the drug trade, and/or possibly expanding his alleged ties with weapons dealers. But those were just shots in the dark. To Aaron's surprise, Tanner didn't flinch at the question. Instead he smiled, leaning over the table and said, "What if I told you that I'm going to be a billionaire?"

"I'd say you were full of shit."

"What if I told you that I'd bring you in on it, if you wanted?"

Aaron's stomach twisted at the proposal. Here it was, the moment he'd been planning on since leaving the Corps to accept this mission. It had all seemed hypothetical then, and a way that he might be able to do the right thing and possibly help his brother. Tanner was his brother, after all, and what brother would wish ill on his sibling?

Tanner continued. "I know you may not like it, but everything you've done in Seattle has helped me get to where I am now. So let's just call it payback, me saying thanks for doing the hard part."

Aaron knew he was in the middle of one of those crucial moments, where what he said in response and how he acted could tip his brother off to his true motives. He couldn't look too anxious or Tanner might suspect his duplicity. But he also couldn't be too flippant, or his brother might rescind his offer. Aaron decided to go right down the middle.

"It sounds like bullshit to me, but I'll help if I can."

Tanner grinned.

"Okay. Here's what I need you to do."

CHAPTER SEVENTEEN

At first, I made my way back toward Tanner's place. Then, as I stared out the bus window, I thought better of my plan. What if Singleton told Tanner I was coming? And what if the cops were waiting at his apartment?

I couldn't take that chance. It wouldn't help anyone if I got caught. As far as I knew, I was a fugitive from the law. It wasn't the first time, and the realization didn't faze me. It was easy to stay under the radar when you knew what you were doing.

What bothered me was that I'd been so close to finding out what Singleton was up to. If those security guards hadn't shown up when they did, I might've had it all. A guy like Singleton would give up his own mother to save himself from physical pain. I couldn't go back to the hospital. Maybe Aaron could track down where the guy lived and we could pay him a visit.

It was the only thing I could think of.

I closed my eyes and tried to mimic the exercise I'd done in bed early that morning. Blocking out the sound of the revving bus engine and the chattering Chinese women across the aisle, I re-centered my focus. I didn't know if Singleton had been lying about the drugs, but I promised myself that I wouldn't try that route again, even if not taking those drugs meant I experienced more pain and coping required a lot more mental effort. I was now determined to do things the natural way, the way people had dealt with adversity for centuries before apothecaries developed the first mind-deadening drugs.

In and out my breath flowed, and once again I settled deeper into my core. The familiar crosshairs appeared in my mind's eye, and I let the image lull me into a half-sleep.

AARON'S HOUSE was empty when I arrived. On the ferry ride to Bainbridge Island, I had the opportunity to think. I was still grappling with the lingering effects of the drugs, or withdrawal, or whatever was twisting my brain, but at least I'd gotten a measure of my inner composure back. It was like finding insidious venom that had to be extracted slowly and with great care. I saw the venom now and was absolutely confident I could beat it.

While I waited for Aaron, I did some light calisthenics, anything to get my blood flowing. The adrenaline helped me think with the added benefit of making me laser focused. Through the push-ups and sit ups, I calculated our chances of success. Tanner was a cunning enemy, a true chameleon. I could respect that. I understood it more than others. I knew what it was to have two faces, and The Beast growled in agreement.

What did a guy like Tanner want? Money was the obvious answer, but it seemed too easy. Power was the next step, the logical progression of ambitious men. But that still didn't seem right. Up to this point, Tanner had done everything he could to stay out of the spotlight. It was possible that his

cloak of anonymity was about to be cast aside. Anything was
possible, and yet, I thought there was something more
behind Tanner's ambitions.

———

THE OUTBOARD ENGINE of the Boston Whaler rumbled as
the boat pulled up to the small pier. Aaron Gray reversed the
throttle and nestled the boat right up to the rubber edge. He
hopped off the side and pulled the drifting vessel back in,
tying off the bow line and then the stern.

He'd breathed a sigh of relief when he saw the lights on at
his house. While he'd wanted to make it back earlier, his
brother kept him busy all day. The tiny glimpse into Tanner's
world – and that was all it had been, tiny – raised the hairs on
the back of Aaron's neck. There was much more to Tanner
than he'd ever imagined.

NCIS painted his brother as a smart crook who'd
somehow figured out a temporary way to remain the anony-
mous head of a criminal enterprise. What Aaron had seen
was a stark contrast to the small-time dealer Tanner was
supposed to be.

They were wrong. So very wrong.

Aaron's image of Tanner had changed. He'd always considered his brother a cool character, calm under fire, and at ease
when others might flee. But now he'd seen part of the truth.
The closest comparison Aaron could come up with now were
those Silicon Valley CEOs, the young and driven individuals
racing for venture capital money and a windfall IPO. That
was the vibe Tanner gave off the second he'd opened up. It
was like Aaron was seeing the real Tanner for the first time.

Aaron shook his head as he snatched the keys from the
boat, and checked the lines one last time. He didn't have all
the answers yet; he was not even close. It was more like he'd

felt the first tremor from a coming earthquake. The only question now was whether he and Daniel could do anything to stop it and the collateral damage Tanner was sure to cause.

———

TANNER COULDN'T BE HAPPIER. After years of keeping his feelings and ambitions from his brother, he'd finally found an opening. Things were coming together, and the fact that he would have Aaron along for the ride made it that much better. Having a secret life was never easy, despite how easy Tanner made it look. One of the aspects of the Marine Corps that he'd missed was the feeling of brotherhood; that no matter what, there was someone there next to you, sharing the good times and bad. In the Corps, someone always had your back.

He'd longed for that in a hidden part of his soul. Tanner was introspective enough to understand that he'd hidden that need from himself, and just like the founder of a start-up business, he'd ignored the need for honest and personal relationships. It wasn't ego that got him there; it was necessity.

But now he needed someone on his side that he could trust. When he'd first encountered Daniel Briggs, Tanner thought that maybe the famed sniper could fill that role. It was one of the reasons he'd saved Briggs from the juice room; that, and that fact that he couldn't leave a fellow Marine behind. After all, the man was a hero, someone who'd walked through the fires of hell and come out relatively unscathed. The cracks in Daniel's armor had shown quickly, and Tanner was glad for that. It was another affirmation that what he was doing was needed.

Tanner might be another kind of hero, and even if no one else in the world knew, Tanner would.

He adjusted his tie and looked at his image in the full-length mirror. Tanner liked what he saw, another facade, one that would serve him well, and seal the deal of a lifetime.

———

I'D HEARD the boat on its approach, and watched from the shadows as it docked. Aaron trudged towards the house, and I met him halfway.

"Where'd you get the boat?" I asked.

"Rented it."

"For what?"

"Figured we might need it," Aaron said cryptically. He looked deflated, and he walked past me into the house.

I let him grab a beer and settle into one of the living room armchairs before continuing my question barrage.

"Did you see your brother?"

Aaron nodded, still deep in thought. He was staring at the coffee table, taking measured sips of his Budweiser.

"I went by his place," I said, "and I paid the VA doctor a little visit."

"I heard," Aaron said without looking up.

"What else did you hear?"

Aaron's face twisted with frustration. "We were all wrong, about the drug dealing, about Tanner, about everything."

"I know."

That made him look up.

"What do you know?"

I thought back to Dr. Singleton's office and the brief conversation we'd had.

"This is bigger than you thought," I said.

Aaron nodded.

CHAPTER EIGHTEEN

The dinner had gone well. Tanner loved that journalists belonged to a handful of professions, other than government agencies, that didn't have to identify their sources. It was the ultimate loophole and Tanner loved that it allowed him to skirt the law, or at least twist it to his advantage.

He waved to the taxi cab while Emily Gill, an up-and-coming reporter with the Washington Post, was staring at the notebook in her hands. After he'd convinced her that he wasn't a fraud, and shown her the pictures to prove it, she hadn't stopped writing the whole meal. Ms. Gill had plenty to think about. Tanner knew she'd win big on this one. It could be the home run that would catapult her into the big leagues.

Tanner wasn't interested in Emily Gill, even if she was single and hot in her own literary way. His sights were set far ahead, and nothing would deter him from his course. He'd laid every brick by hand, carefully and with forethought he considered visionary.

Now it was time to meet another visionary, one who would not only benefit from Tanner's exploits, but who could catapult his plan to the next level, and a man who his most important contact had recommended personally.

The former Marine waved one final goodbye to the cab. The night was young and his next appointment was waiting. No sense letting a billionaire get his panties in a bunch.

————

HOWARD BISHOP STARED out the floor-to-ceiling windows of the hotel penthouse suite and frowned at the view. He hated coming to Seattle. It was so dreary. Sure, the city had come into its own recently, but it still felt like a Podunk town to him. After all, he spent his days hopping from New York City to Paris and Hong Kong. Those were cities, pinnacles of humanity and shining beacons of immense wealth. Anything else was just low class and beneath him.

But this trip was necessary. If he had any chance of taking his company to stratospheric levels with the returns to match, this was it. The money was so close he could taste it. There had been big wins in his past – enough to make him a wealthy man – but this play could make the previous gains look amateur.

Howard Bishop wanted to play with the elite of the elite, men like Bill Gates and Carlos Slim, men who'd revolutionized their fields. They had come out the other end with cement trucks full of money. That was what Bishop wanted, enough wealth that he could erase the memories of his childhood, years spent scraping by, begging just to have a bite to eat.

He pushed the recollection away as soon as it came. Bishop hadn't become the man he was by dwelling on the past. Yes, he'd learned from his days hopping from orphanage to shelter and then back to another orphanage, but he knew he was stronger for it. He was a self-made man, something many of the world's wealthiest men and women could never say for themselves. He was Howard Bishop, a giant among men, or at least very soon to be.

The penthouse chime sounded and he walked to the door. He'd let his confused assistant take the night off, something he rarely did. Tonight was about secrecy of the highest order. No one must know, not even his always-tightening inner circle.

When he opened the door, he was surprised to see a young man standing in front of him. He looked like a thousand eager young executives who'd tried and failed to get Bishop's attention over the years.

"Mr. Bishop," the young man said, not bothering to extend a hand. Part of Bishop was repulsed by the lack of civility, but then he realized it was for the best. Best not to even touch the bringer of such vital tidings.

"And what should I call you?" Bishop asked.

"Tom would be fine."

Both men eyed each other for a long moment. Bishop was accustomed to these staring contests, which he always won. It surprised him that "Tom" did not flinch; he didn't move a muscle. That made Bishop's hands tingle with anticipation.

"Come in, please," Bishop said courteously.

Tom followed him into the luxury suite and refused a drink when offered.

"I'm sure you'd like to get right to business," Tom said.

Bishop nodded and poured himself a stiff drink.

"Do you do much of this type of work?" Bishop asked, curious about Tom's experience in such affairs.

"Not specifically."

"And how do I know that I can trust you?"

Tom smiled, a glimmer of deviousness in his eyes. "I think you know why you can trust me, Mr. Bishop."

"The money," Bishop guessed. Tom nodded. "And how do I know the information you've promised is mine alone?"

"I'm a man of my word, Mr. Bishop," Tom said.

Bishop couldn't help but laugh.

"You're an interesting man, Tom. Very interesting. Are you sure I can't get you a drink?"

"I'll be happy to have one after we've settled what I've come here to discuss."

"Very well, tell me your plan."

Howard Bishop found it hard not to let his jaw drop on more than one occasion. As Tom outlined what he'd already accomplished, careful not to give too much away, Bishop found himself liking Tom more by the moment. The young man was truly masterful, a cunning devil. Bishop wondered if there were more opportunities like the one Tom had uncovered. It made Bishop salivate just thinking of it.

But he wasn't going to let on how enticing Tom's tale was. That just wasn't Bishop's way.

"I'm not sure this is worth the amount we first discussed," Bishop said, looking toward the cloud covered Seattle skyline.

Again, Tom did not flinch.

"And I'm sure that Stanley Rosenbaum would love to pay me as much, if not more, if I decided to pay him a visit."

Bishop flinched despite himself. Stanley Rosenbaum was ever the thorn in his side. They'd been acquaintances in their early twenties, and had even been friends at one time, but that changed once the climb to the top began in earnest. While the media loved Rosenbaum, and considered him some kind of modern day saint, they vilified Bishop as he slugged it out in court and countered with expensive appeals. Every time he thought of Stanley Rosenbaum with his perfect wife and perfect kids, Bishop wanted to slam his fist into a wall.

He was sure that Tom recognized the blood rush to his

face, but if he did, he said nothing. Instead he sat impassive, waiting for Bishop's next counter. It was unsettling to a man who was used to having the upper hand, or at least pretending he did, as a means to topple his next foe.

"Look, Mr. Bishop, this is all very time sensitive. I don't want to go to Rosenbaum. I'd much prefer to do business with you and make us both very wealthy."

"I'm already wealthy," Bishop said. The words sounded lame even to him.

"I know the Feds are all over your company, Mr. Bishop. How would you like to make that all go away? Instead of being treated like the pariah, you could be the hero."

Bishop liked the sound of that. Even though he would never admit it, he wanted to be looked upon like his chief rival. Didn't everyone want to be seen as the hero, not the villain?

"If you give me a couple of days, you won't have to worry about your competition for as long you're alive," Tom said, grinning like a co-conspirator.

"And all you want in return is a small percentage."

Tom raised his hands like he was conceding defeat.

"I'm not a greedy man, Mr. Bishop. You and your company get to keep the lion's share. I just want to be comfortable."

Bishop snorted. "And you're confident billions will keep you comfortable?"

Tom smirked. "It's a start."

———

Tanner felt like skipping. It took every ounce of self-control he had to keep his smile in check. He nodded to the hotel concierge as he passed through the lobby. Once outside, he exhaled in relief. It was drizzling, but Tanner barely noticed. He felt like he was above it all.

The meeting with Bishop had been the final test, and he'd come out on top. The CEO would never know all the details, and when he'd pressed for more, Tanner explained that it was in his best interest not to know certain aspects of what was about to happen. More importantly for Tanner, he couldn't show all his cards to Bishop lest the greedy bastard attempt to do it on his own.

That was impossible without all the evidence, and Tanner had already prepared his own insurance policy should Bishop at any point renege on their agreement.

The misty Seattle air couldn't dampen Tanner's spirits. In fact, he thought his senses felt heightened, like he'd somehow obtained a higher level of awareness. He wondered if having billions in your bank account made food taste better. Of course it did. Billions made everything better.

CHAPTER NINETEEN

Senator Janet Lasky was a first-term senator from Washington State. She'd gotten both her undergrad and law degrees from the University of Washington. She was one of those rare Democrats who somehow straddled the center aisle of politics. Her political stance was very likely influenced by the views of her late husband. He had been a staunch Republican, the conservative principles firmly cemented into his being due to his time in the Army. Probably more influential had been the chosen path of her two boys, Ray and Kenneth. They'd taken after their father in many ways, including enlisting in the Army as soon as they'd turned eighteen. But she believed they'd inherited a piece of her bleeding heart, and had always understood the plight of those less fortunate.

Senator Lasky touched the faces of her two boys in the picture that took center stage on her desk. It was from a sun-soaked week at their favorite Oregon beach. The trip had been an annual pilgrimage for the three after her husband died. It was their favorite place, somewhere that the calls from her ever-growing law practice could not reach, and a remote hideaway where the boys forgot their teenage worries and once again connected like only brothers do.

They were gone now, taken from her in the prime of their lives. Her beautiful boys lived on only in pictures now, ripped from her life like a trick from the heavens. Kenneth had been killed by an IED in Iraq. Ray had taken it the worst, and for a time had to be admitted to a military mental health institution. He'd emerged a different person, his familiar laugh now muted by the cruelty of war.

After that, Ray left the Army on full disability, but refused to come home. She hadn't been a senator at the time, and yet, her life during that period was more hectic while her private law firm dominated the Seattle landscape. Her schedule showed it.

She regretted not devoting more time to her grieving son. At the time it was all she could do to keep moving forward, despite the pain. It was bad enough to lose your husband, but to outlive your child? It was unnatural.

And then Ray took his own life. She'd been in court when the call came. Her housekeeper called providing a heads-up that police were at the front gate. At first, Lasky thought it had something to do with one of her past clients. When they informed her of her son's death, all she could do was scream at them to leave her alone.

She went back to work the day after she buried her son. The three most important men in her life were gone. It took months for her to feel anything again. After the fog cleared, all she'd felt was rage. It was that rage that catapulted her from high-powered attorney to toppling an incumbent U.S. Senator. She'd done it in honor of her boys' memories, and the people of the State of Washington had swept her in because of it.

Ever since taking her oath, she'd spent every moment she could fighting for the rights and the welfare of military veterans. She'd gone after the VA for their incompetency and attacked fellow politicians for their lack of oversight. Everyone knew her reasons. Senator Lasky had nothing to lose. Her life was made up of battles now, and there wasn't a day that passed where her office didn't rail against some foe.

For the Senator, the quiet times were the hardest. She could go days without thinking of her own pain, but it always came back. So, as she sat at her desk, stroking the smiling images of her dead sons, Senator Lasky hoped she was doing enough.

THE RINGING PHONE snapped her back to the present. She hit the speaker button. "Yes?"

"Senator, I've got Howard Bishop on the phone," her secretary, Rhonda, said.

"It's a little late, Francine. Could you tell him I'll call him back tomorrow?"

Senator Lasky didn't want to talk with Howard Bishop. The man had an ego that rivaled Napoleon's, and his reputation was far from where he truly believed it to be. He'd been hammering on her door since she'd entered office. He always said they should partner in order to help her constituency. Lasky doubted that very much, and made it plain that her time in the Senate, no matter how short, would not be shadowed by money-laced deals with corporations lobbying for a senator's ear. She had one mission in life, and that was to help men and women like her two sons.

"He says it's urgent, Senator," the secretary pressed, her tone cutting through Lasky's annoyance. Her secretary was as ardent about protecting her boss's time as the senator was about fighting for military veterans.

"Okay, but make sure I'm not on for more than five

minutes." She heard Rhonda chuckle, and then the line clicked over. "Senator Lasky."

"Thank you for taking the time to speak with me, Senator." Bishop's voice was syrupy polite. Lasky cringed.

"What can I do for you, Mr. Bishop?"

"A little bird told me that you've been working with Doreen Davis."

"It's not a state secret, Mr. Bishop."

Senator Lasky jumped to the most logical assumption. Howard Bishop had heard about the coming boon for Palacor International, the company led by CEO Doreen Davis, and wanted to stick his head in for a peek. Palacor was one of Bishop's main rivals, and he'd made it plain that he wanted to take the top spot from the enigmatic Davis.

In Davis, Senator Lasky saw a true equal, another female fighting for what was right, leading the charge in an industry dominated by men. They'd bonded immediately, and only strengthened their working relationship by both women contributing significant time and energy. Just the fact that Bishop was wasting her time was enough to make the senator want to hang up the phone, but to bring her friend into the fray...

"What is it you need, Mr. Bishop?" she asked coldly.

"I wanted to call and warn you, Senator. You might want to reconsider your relationship with Ms. Davis."

Lasky bristled. "Are you threatening me, Mr. Bishop?"

The senator was no amateur when it came to receiving threats. It came with the territory, both as an attorney and as a politician. She escaped much of the usual nonsense during her run as an Independent, but there were still the kooks who liked to level biased barbs or political colleagues who had nothing better to do than throw jagged stones on morning talk shows.

"I'm sorry if it sounds that way, Senator, because that was the last thing on my mind."

Lasky doubted that very much. Bishop's penchant for intimidation was well known. He would've made a powerful politician if he'd wanted.

"I suggest you get to the point," Lasky said, her voice cutting through the phone like a scythe.

"Make sure you get a copy of the Washington Post tomorrow morning. Once you've had a chance to read it, call me, and I'll get you out of the mess."

Lasky was about to reply, but the phone went dead. All she could do was stare at it. Confusion turned to a morsel of fear in the pit of her stomach. What was Howard Bishop up to?

CHAPTER TWENTY

What do you do when you know *something* is going to happen, but you don't know what *it* is? Aaron and I both knew that Tanner was in the final implementation stage of whatever he'd concocted. He'd let Aaron in on such a tiny view of the master plan that it was impossible to predict which way things might go.

We were unanimous on one point. Tanner had to be stopped. Hitting too early would spook him, so we needed to let things roll for the time being. The question now was how far to let it go, and if we would even have a chance to stop it once Tanner pressed GO.

"So we know this has something to do with drugs," Aaron was saying, repeating what we'd already gone over too many times to count. He had a huge plug of tobacco in his cheek to ward off much-needed sleep. I did my best without even a cup of coffee. I wasn't going to put any mood-altering substance in my body. It was close to dawn, and we were no closer to solving the riddle than when we'd started.

"I think we should get some sleep and then see what the morning brings," I said, yawning into my hand. There was a time to brainstorm and there was a time to sleep. I needed the latter.

"I'm too wired. You go ahead. I'll come get you in a couple of hours."

The weariness hit me all at once, and I dragged myself to the bedroom. My eyes closed at the same time as the door behind me, and I slipped under the covers, blissfully unaware of the pending events.

THE KNOCKING INTRUDED like a waiter dropping a tray full of china. My head was pounding when I cracked open my eyes and remembered where I was.

"Yeah?" I said, propping myself up on one elbow and rubbing my eyes with my hand.

"Can I come in?" Aaron asked.

I sat up and switched on the bedside lamp, squinting as the light assaulted my eyes. Padding to the door, I wondered what time it was. It felt like I'd only been asleep for maybe an hour. I unlocked and opened the door. Aaron was holding an oversized travel mug of coffee. His stimulant of choice was a cheek full of chew.

"You need to come see this," he said, heading back toward the living room before I could question him.

The television was on when I entered and it took a second for me to figure out what was happening. Bold white lettering announced, "Palacor International Linked to Possible Veteran Abuse."

I didn't have a clue what Palacor International was, but I froze before asking Aaron about the firm. There, on the screen, was a familiar sight, something I only remembered in pieces, and now it was there for the world to see. The video was jittery, and it bounced around a bit. It looked like the kind of quality we got with pirated movies while stationed in

Iraq. The lighting sucked, but it was impossible to miss the rows of cots. Each cot held an unconscious, blanket-covered form. Every person had an IV stand next to them, and an IV line was running from a bag, disappearing under the cot blanket.

I glanced at Aaron, but he was glued to the screen. The video minimized, sent to the background as a news anchor appeared in the foreground.

"As we mentioned earlier in the hour, Washington Post reporter, Emily Gill, broke the story in this morning's edition. Ms. Gill's exposé on pharmaceutical giant Palacor International describes a series of hidden testing facilities used to examine a new Palacor International drug that is currently going through FDA trials. According to Gill, these facilities were not sanctioned by the FDA, and are essentially secret testing grounds. But what takes this story from incredible to sinister is that Ms. Gill asserts that these facilities are conducting this alleged testing on military veterans who are quite possibly sufferers of PTSD."

The television went quiet, although the anchor was still talking. Aaron was holding the remote in his hand. His face was pale as he continued to stare at the screen. I imagined what he must be thinking, that the police and the FBI were probably already suiting up. There would be raids that day if the locations could be found.

"I screwed up," he said, his voice detached and empty.

"We didn't know this was going to happen."

Aaron shook his head. "I should have known."

It was just bad luck and bad timing. I was about to ask how he could've known, when he said, "It was me. I was the one that took those videos. I was the one who gave them to Tanner."

————

HOWARD BISHOP COULDN'T STOP WATCHING. He only wished he could be a fly on the wall in Doreen Davis's corporate headquarters. Davis had to be scrambling, and Bishop relished the thought of the do-gooder getting battered. The media was having a field day, and pretty soon the Feds would be in on the bloodbath, too. It was too good.

The kid said there would be a surprise, but Bishop never thought it would be this big. Palacor stock would crumble and the CEO of Bishop Pharmaceuticals would sit back and laugh. As the number three drug company in the world, Bishop Pharmaceuticals had much to gain. Palacor had win after win in their corner, while Bishop had only managed a handful of second-rate innovations. That would all change.

With Palacor crippled, and most likely under federal investigation, Bishop could swoop in and present a solution. It wouldn't be an easy fight, and the world would take time to forgive big pharma for the sins of one of its members, but Bishop had faith. Better yet, he had a secret weapon in his corner that would help him fulfill Palacor's broken promises. It would provide America, and eventually the world, with an answer to one of its most pressing problems.

He knew the calls would be coming soon. News outlets would want his official statement. He would have his best writers on the task, instructing them to craft a message that provided solace for the injured parties and a promise he would be instrumental in righting the ship. He would appear stoic yet humble, ashamed yet resolute. His time was coming, and it was all Howard Bishop could do not to pop the champagne just yet.

———

THE PHONE CALLS to the senator's office poured in like a broken dam spewing forth its long-held contents. Her constituents wanted answers. They knew about her work with Palacor; they'd listened to her promises.

Senator Lasky cursed the situation and cursed Howard Bishop. He had to be part of this. Somehow he'd been involved.

But it was hard to ignore the facts as they played out on news channels across the nation. She imagined her own son in one of those disgusting rooms, hooked up to an IV with the clear logo of Palacor displayed on one side. It reminded her of the scene in *The Matrix*, where humans were kept alive in fluid-filled capsules, providing living energy for the robot lords of the future until they were no longer needed.

Lasky tried to push the image from her mind. Then she did what she'd always done since those first days in court when a case seemed on the verge of collapse and everyone else envisioned pending doom: Lasky stepped back from it all, like her spirit left her corporeal form. She let the details flow like a black and white motion picture, slides clicking one by one. She sorted through them and discarded what was not needed.

Lasky emerged from her trance with two certainties. First, no matter what the truth was behind the allegations, Davis and Palacor were in for the fight of their lives. The images were too vivid, and the Washington Post article mentioned further evidence linking the drug company to the illicit affair. Investigations would lead to lawsuits. Lawsuits would cost money, and more importantly, time. As any smart politician would do, Lasky had to distance herself from the upheaval, lest she be sucked into the mire.

The second thing she knew for certain was that she would never stop fighting. She'd put in too much time to tuck tail and run. Her path had been set the day her son committed suicide. Lasky felt an urgent need to help the other young men and women who thought that taking one's life was the only solution. At that moment, she knew what she had to do. She knew there was one person who had the answers she needed.

With the same determination she'd used to trounce an eight-term senator, Senator Janet Lasky picked up the phone and asked her secretary to patch her through to Howard Bishop.

———

TANNER GRAY WATCHED the mayhem unfold at a coffee shop around the corner from his apartment. The Washington Post reporter had done well. She'd crafted a compelling narrative, the details of which he'd provided, but that she'd carved into a must-read story on good versus evil. With America at the height of its pro-armed forces jubilation, the thought of an underhanded drug company taking advantage of wounded warriors cut right to the heart of even the most liberal pundits.

To every red-blooded American, Palacor was now the enemy. It needed to be dismantled, piece by piece, man by man. Never mentioned were the drugs that the innovative company had spent billions perfecting to help people all over the world. Not once did a reporter discuss the millions Palacor gave each year to charities and to the indigent.

Tanner thought back to his weeks at boot camp. Would his drill instructors ever have guessed he would be capable of this? Sure he'd gotten a few lucky breaks, the biggest being that the illegal drug outfit he'd targeted for takeover had actually gotten their hands on Palacor's medication. But he'd pulled the chessboard out from under their amateur scheme. Preying on disabled veterans was small time. Getting those veterans to sign away their benefits and enlist in a new army of near-constant sedation was little league compared to what he had planned.

As always, he'd play it from the sidelines, the hidden mongoose in a den of snakes. The video had been a last minute idea. It turned out to be the killing blow for Palacor. If a picture was worth a thousand words, Tanner figured a video was worth a million or, maybe in this case, a billion and change.

The day would see much finger-pointing, and in the end Palacor closed ranks and braced for impact. It was all they could do. They'd never seen the salvo coming. And how could they? A few lost shipments from their labs in the Philippines would take months to trace. So for now the world watched the feeding frenzy, and Tanner moved on toward his closing tasks.

CHAPTER TWENTY-ONE

As the morning dragged on, Aaron's mood went from sour to shit. He'd checked in with his NCIS cohorts, who informed him agents were coming to help with damage control.

"They think we waited too long," Aaron said, throwing the pouch of Redman tobacco in the air. "They're not wrong."

"But what can they do now?" I asked. I didn't want to be around for the unhappy reunion. The last thing I needed was to be on NCIS's radar. They were very good at what they did, and if they wanted, they could pull every bit of my military record. Hell, they probably already had.

Aaron shrugged, tossing the pouch up again and narrowly missing the fan spinning languidly overhead.

"I bet they bring me in and try to do the same with Tanner."

That was the smart thing to do. NCIS wasn't about to get pulled into the swirling controversy of Palacor's downfall. If the public found out that NCIS had a man on the inside who knew what was going on, and that they had done nothing about it... Well, it wouldn't only be Palacor in the crosshairs;

every federal agency from the FBI to the DEA would pounce on the NCIS.

"How much time do we have?"

"They said they'd be here tonight," Aaron said. The tobacco pouch slapped into his hand and he turned to face me. "We don't have much time."

"What are you thinking?"

The spark in his eyes had returned.

"We need to talk to Tanner."

Before I could agree, his cell phone rang. Aaron glanced at the screen and cursed under his breath.

"Who is it?" I asked.

"It's the guy who runs distribution, the one who set up the IV centers."

He'd told me all about the guy. He went by the name Ulysses, although Aaron was pretty sure that wasn't his real name. Of mixed Asian and Caucasian descent, the ring leader sounded like a real piece of work. In a world where tough and smart ruled, Aaron said that Ulysses took the blue ribbon prize.

"Yeah?" Aaron said, answering the call. I couldn't hear, but I did see Aaron's face harden. "Okay, I'll be there."

Once the call had ended, I asked, "What did he say?"

"He wants to meet. Said he has some questions for me."

"Don't go."

"But what if he knows something that could help us?"

"It's not worth it," I said. "We should find Tanner." I could see by the look on Aaron's face he was unconvinced of my strategy.

"I'm going," he said, finally, already heading for the door.

"I'll go with you."

"It's better if you stay. You're right, it could be dangerous."

"Thanks for the concern, *Dad*, but if I wanted safe I wouldn't have stuck around."

He stopped and looked back. Then he gave me a nod. "Okay. Let's take the boat."

WE TIED the boat off in the shadow of a huge cruise ship and next to some rich man's yacht. We were a few blocks north of Aaron's meeting place with his boss at the outdoor park adjacent to the Seattle Aquarium. The plan was that I would go in first and scope the place out. If I spotted an ambush, I would double back and warn Aaron. If I didn't, I'd just find a place to hunker down and watch Aaron's back.

It was one of those beautiful sunny days in Seattle, and it seemed like every tourist and local saw it as their duty to soak in every last ray. The sidewalks and pathways were clogged with walkers and bikers, mothers and fathers yelling at kids to watch where they were going.

It was perfect for me. I weaved through the throng, the familiar press of bodies welcoming me back to civilization. When I made it to the aquarium, I spotted a row of vendors under bright white tents next to the water. The guy selling coffee was smack in the middle, and I continued to make my way there as I scanned the area.

I didn't see any obvious threats, but that meant little. With this many people clogging the sidewalks, even a gorilla could've found a spot to hide. I'd been waiting in line at least five minutes when I saw Ulysses. He was coming up one of the sets of stairs, alone. The guy fit Aaron's description to a T. His Asian ancestry gave him that angular look that could grace the cover of a magazine, while his fair hair gave a nod to his Caucasian descent. Even though he wore khaki pants and a button-down shirt, I surmised he would be just as comfortable in either jeans or a tuxedo. He simply had that suave look of a player.

With a toothpick in his mouth, he looked bored. As I

placed my order at the coffee stand, I watched Ulysses pull a phone out of his pocket and take a call. It didn't last long, and by the time I had my coffee in hand, and went to find a spot with a view, he was sitting on a concrete ledge, chatting amiably with a pair of pretty young girls.

I sipped my coffee and continued my surveillance until Aaron came into view. He didn't make a direct line to his boss, but I did see Ulysses zero in on Aaron. It was all very casual, like he didn't have a care in the world.

After hitting the same coffee stand as I had, Aaron made his way over to Ulysses. That's when the shot rang out.

————

AARON GRAY HAD COME to respect the man he only knew as Ulysses. Drug dealer seemed too simple a description for the man. By the way he talked, Ulysses had higher aspirations. He wanted to take his operation to a higher level, and in many ways it mirrored Tanner Gray's plan, even if neither man knew it. Just the fact that Ulysses had somehow forged relationships within the VA and the banking world spoke to his talents.

For months, Aaron had only caught glimpses of Ulysses, but the Asian-American had an eye for talent, and soon Aaron was formally introduced to his boss. Aaron had walked away impressed. Ulysses cut a fine Silicone Valley figure, even though his chosen profession threw him in direct contact with the worst of the criminal underworld. The other thing Aaron had realized from that meeting was that Ulysses was not a man to piss off.

Ulysses locked eyes with Aaron, who was walking over to him with his cup of coffee. Every fiber in the Marine's body felt tingly, just like those days in the Corps, when any patrol might end up in an ambush. Those were the best days of his life, when the only thing that mattered was accomplishing the mission and taking care of his fellow Marines. He'd been one of the best, a warrior trained for war and peace. While he would've been just as content handing out aid packages to starving refugees, it was something about youth that yearned for the thrill of battle.

He felt that same excitement as he neared Ulysses, the crowd parting like they were funneling him to his waiting boss. Maybe this was it. Maybe this was where they parted ways, when Ulysses said the hammer was about to deliver a death blow to his business. It could go the other way, and Ulysses could put a gun in his face and demand to know about Aaron's involvement in the leaked video. He wouldn't put it past the good-looking leader. He would've done the same, starting with the new guy, who'd risen so quickly within his organization.

Aaron nodded and stepped closer to Ulysses, thinking about taking a seat next to him on the concrete wall. That never happened, because as soon as he made the move, a gunshot thundered from the crowd.

———

THE GUNSHOT SPOOKED the crowd like a herd of cattle. Some ducked for cover and others bolted. Lost in the scramble were Ulysses and Aaron, and I crashed into the screaming crowd to reach them. I caught a glimpse of bright red from where the two men had been, until then the crowd carried me along with its tidal wave of panicked people. Eventually, I lost sight of the meeting spot.

Police sirens pierced the terror of the crowd, and I knew it would be a matter of minutes before officers would be swarming the small park. Forward I pushed, toppling a huge father carrying his young son under one arm. I heard him yell at me, but I kept going, throwing elbows when I had to, just doing my best to swim forward.

I was almost there when I felt a blunt stab in the side. For a split second, I thought the big guy I'd knocked over had somehow caught up to me, but when I glanced to the side I was shocked to see a familiar face. Tanner Gray had a coat draped over his arm, and that arm, I knew, held a pistol that was jabbed into my ribs.

"Go the other way," he said, pointing with his head the way the crowd was moving. I chanced a look over to where Aaron had been, but Tanner pressed harder and said, "Move, now."

I nodded and turned that way. No sooner had I started on the divergent path, until someone knocked into me. I went with the shove and tumbled to the ground. Inside, The Beast took my cue and gladly gained control of my body. Head tucked, and torso folding, I fell as my alter ego rolled me into a somersault, and then, like a gymnast on a tumbling mat, sprang back the way I'd come with the agility of a jungle cat.

My fists shot out, connecting a solid double blow in the middle of Tanner's face. He staggered back, one hand still holding the weapon and the other reaching for his battered eye socket, which was streaming blood. Tanner must have heard the wailing of the sirens through the pounding in his head because he suddenly cradled the coat-covered pistol to his chest, and sprinted in the opposite direction.

I took one step toward Tanner until I remembered Aaron, who was probably lying in a pool of blood, courtesy of his own brother. Police be damned, I had to see it for myself. I growled with The Beast and leaped over a young woman who was rocking back and forth on the ground. She didn't look hurt, just stuck to her place from shock and fright.

There was the blood again, just a peek through the crowd,

and then someone whistled. I thought it was the cops, but was relieved to see Aaron running toward me.

"You okay?" I asked when we reached each other.

"Yeah, but we need to get out of here."

The crowd was thinning now, most of them having found cover or an early trip home. I followed Aaron as he blended in with the last stragglers, even taking one arm each of an old man who was hobbling away from the scene. My last look back gave me a perfect view of the blood-spattered face of Ulysses, his body splayed unceremoniously over the concrete wall. His lifeless eyes bulged, seeming to follow us as we hurried on our way.

CHAPTER TWENTY-TWO

Senator Janet Lasky felt bitter bile hit the back of her mouth as Howard Bishop walked into the private dining room. She was on her third drink and had no intention of stopping. If Bishop was her last resort, Lasky could afford to get a little drunk.

"Good evening, Senator," Bishop said upon entering. If he was surprised that she didn't rise to greet him, he played it off well, motioning to the waiter for a drink.

The place had been his idea, and he was almost forty minutes late. That only added to Lasky's annoyance and her need to coat her distaste with another glass of Chardonnay.

"I'm sorry to keep you waiting. I had some last minute issues to attend to."

She nodded and guzzled the rest of her drink. Lasky reminded herself that she was the one with all the power. Bishop was a male chauvinist of the highest order, and Lasky would have to keep a semblance of calm to deal with the insufferable braggart.

"You said you could help, so I came."

The waiter was back and she got his attention by waving

the wine glass in the air. He snatched it deftly and left to fetch a refill.

"I know you don't see it this way, but we're on the same side this time," Bishop said, sipping from the glass of dark booze.

Lasky sneered, then relaxed, reminding herself that she had to maintain control. Maybe food would do her some good and maybe no more wine.

"You've burned Palacor and now you want to step in as the savior," she guessed aloud.

To this Bishop actually smiled.

"Believe me if you want, but I didn't have a thing to do with outing Palacor."

"I find that very hard to believe."

He nodded his agreement, and then said slowly, "Haven't you ever caught wind of something before it actually happened?"

Senator Lasky considered his last statement. Of course she'd been privy to information and intelligence before a big event. It came with the territory of owning a successful law practice, and especially with her new career in the United States Senate.

"You know I have," she said, quieting as the waiter stepped in and laid the newly-filled wine glass in front of her. "I think I'd like to order now."

The waiter nodded and looked to Bishop.

Without looking up, Bishop said, "Tell Pierre I have a special guest." The waiter left with a flourish and Bishop smiled. "Pierre makes the best escargot. You like it, I hope?"

Lasky now realized that what she really needed was bread and water. Her head was starting to spin from the wine.

"That sounds fine," she said.

Howard Bishop grinned, not seeming to notice her slightly diminished facial color. He went on.

"Like I was saying, we're on the same side, Senator. I want what you want, what you've been fighting so hard for since the day you stepped into the Senate."

Lasky wanted to laugh. She held her tongue, even biting it to keep from letting a wine-laced barb fly across the table. After taking a leisurely drink of water, she finally answered.

"Let's say it was coincidence that you knew about Palacor. Let's also assume that you understand what I've been trying to do. Now, what makes you think that I should listen to what you have to say?"

She was regretting ever coming. What she needed now was a hot bath and a good night's rest. The next morning would undoubtedly bring another deluge of phone calls from unhappy constituents. She'd shut off her cell phone for that very reason.

"Senator, how would you like to salvage Palacor's research? In fact, how would you like to see a vast improvement in its formula?"

Now that got Senator Lasky's attention. She'd been to the Palacor labs and read much of the research material herself. It all looked so promising. Even the FDA had given her assurances that an approval was coming. But now the scandal would stop that, possibly negate all the work Doreen Davis and her teams had done. It would even make the loud banging of the war drum Lasky had done on Capitol Hill seem useless. She'd put a lot of time into supporting Palacor and she couldn't imagine all that effort going to waste.

"What are you saying, that I should step in and—"

Bishop interrupted her with a shake of his head. "You don't need to get involved, Senator, at least not yet."

Lasky didn't understand, so she asked the obvious question. "Then how will you do it?"

Bishop sat back and grinned. "I've got the new and improved formula, Senator."

———

COINCIDENCES. In Tanner's world there was no such thing as a coincidence. In fact, the more times people and similar events converged, the more often Tanner tended to stay away. It was too risky for the long term. He'd learned his lesson early that pressing one's luck was never about courage; it was about hedging your bets and stacking the deck in your favor.

He'd gone to the waterfront park to protect his brother. He'd killed Ulysses because a source within the drug dealer's organization happened to be on Tanner's payroll, and that source just happened to tell him that Ulysses meant to kill Aaron.

And then Tanner saw Daniel Briggs, and Daniel was moving towards Aaron. Tanner had done the first thing that had come to mind, protect his little brother. Briggs was a disturbed man, a man whose mind had been twisted by the ravages of war. He had to be there to kill his brother.

But when he weaved through the crowd and confronted the sniper, the cat-like Briggs had somehow snapped surprise back in Tanner's face, just like a case of whiplash. And if that wasn't enough, after stumbling away from the scene, as the police closed in, Tanner saw Briggs and Aaron leaving together. That got his mind working, and as he pressed the bag of ice to his face, Tanner considered his next steps carefully. He wouldn't let another unlikely coincidence fly by.

His rental car turned off the blacktop and onto a gravel road. Dr. Singleton's contemporary home came into view a couple seconds later, all angular wood and illuminated glass. Singleton came from money and hadn't been shy about buying the private residence, well away from the noise of bustling Seattle.

Tanner had only been to the house once, but was familiar enough with the layout that he drove around to the front, the side where a perfect view of Mt. Rainier smiled down on the lucky clear day. Nestled into a grove of trees, the residence provided a quiet getaway.

The front door was unlocked, a fact that annoyed Tanner. He'd told the often-distracted doctor to be careful. The guy didn't have a clue about proper security, and if pressed would probably admit to never using his state-of-the-art alarm system. Tanner locked the door behind him and followed the sounds of Frank Sinatra to the upstairs living area.

When he got to the top of the stairs, Dr. Singleton was dancing slowly, arms stretched out like he was swaying with an invisible partner.

He's so strange, Tanner thought. *So strange, yet so brilliant.*

Tanner rapped his knuckles on the wall and Singleton turned, more curious than alarmed.

"Oh, hello, Tanner."

"Your front door was open."

"Open or unlocked?" Singleton asked, completely serious.

Tanner shook his head. It was useless to get him to worry about personal security.

"If you're done dancing, I'd like to get down to business."

Singleton smiled like a carefree child and headed for one of the pretty, yet totally uncomfortable couches near the windows.

"What happened to your face?" Singleton asked, not really concerned, again just curious.

"Don't worry about it. Look, things are coming together. Do you have the formula ready?"

Singleton smiled again and snapped his fingers. "It's all right here," he said, tapping on his temple.

"Can you put it down on paper? Howard Bishop wants proof."

Singleton's face twisted with annoyance. "Are you sure we should? How do you know he won't go back on his word?"

Singleton didn't know anything about the money Tanner had negotiated. No, the possibility of advancing his own research was more important to the doctor. In exchange for the perfected formula, Singleton would be given a new role within Bishop Pharmaceuticals. He would head up his own development team and conduct the end-stage trials needed for full FDA approval. After that project was completed, Singleton would be let loose on a variety of drugs that would soon be out from patent protection. Reformulating drugs was a common practice in the pharmaceutical industry, but Singleton seemed to have a real knack for building a better product out of other people's inventions. It was a win-win for all involved, and it was sure to make Bishop even more billions.

"The formula is our ticket, Doc. If we don't give him that, we get nothing."

Tanner had seen the results. The effective rate of the drug tested on the small focus group was almost one hundred percent. It would revolutionize that segment of the pharmaceutical industry.

"Fine. Give me a day and I'll have it done," Singleton said, rising from his seat and heading for the kitchen where a timer was dinging. "Are you staying for dinner? I made vegan lasagna."

"I need to get back."

Singleton shrugged and slid the baking dish out of the oven. He didn't pay Tanner any more notice, instead humming along with the next Sinatra tune, already immersed in completing the solo dinner.

Tanner shook his head, and then winced at the pain. With the bag of ice pressed to his bruised face, Tanner left through the front door, careful to lock it on his way out.

CHAPTER TWENTY-THREE

"Are you sure it was him?" Aaron asked.

"Yeah, he looked right at me."

Aaron shook his head. I could imagine that the thought of his brother being at the murder scene was more than a little startling. We'd passed through the police cordon only after a thorough search and careful questioning by the cops. Luckily, neither one of us was armed.

It had taken almost two hours to get back to Aaron's place on Bainbridge Island. The boat ride back had been quiet except for the droning of the outboards. We'd both been too absorbed with our thoughts to say much.

But now that we were on dry land again, it was time to dissect what the hell had happened.

"I don't get it. What was he doing there?" Aaron wondered aloud. "Do you think he followed us?"

"Impossible," I said, even though nothing was impossible. My life was a testament to that fact.

"Do you think he shot Ulysses?"

I shrugged. "It's possible, but like you said, what was he doing there? How did he know?"

Aaron exhaled, letting every ounce of his frustration show. "Either way, my cover is blown. There's no way I can get back in now that Ulysses is dead. They'll think it was me."

"So we go talk to your brother and see what he knows."

The reluctance was stamped on Aaron's face when he looked at me. Once again, we'd been thrust into the abyss of the unknown. In my experience, the best thing to do in times like that was to keep moving. Better to act than to do nothing.

Aaron must have come to the same conclusion because he slapped his thighs and said, "Okay. Let's go see Tanner."

————

HE KNEW it was just a matter of time. If Aaron and Daniel Briggs were working together, he, Tanner Gray, was now their only link. With Ulysses dead, Aaron would have to know that he couldn't go back.

Tanner still didn't know what his brother was up to, and the fact that he was now with Briggs made him more than a little apprehensive. Together they made a formidable team, a team that if pushed the wrong way could bite back, just like Briggs had done at the park. To Briggs, Tanner was the enemy. Now it was up to Tanner to decide if the feeling was mutual, and if he should also consider his brother an accomplice of the enemy.

Tanner wiped the black residue from his fingers onto an old T-shirt, and then clicked the pistol's slide back into place. His heart was heavier than it had been that morning, but Tanner's path was still set. He'd worked too hard to deviate from the plan now. Whatever Aaron and Briggs decided, he would be ready.

But nagging doubt still edged its way into his subconscious, like everything was turning out to be a lie.

THE LIGHTS WERE off in Tanner's apartment as we watched a block away. We'd done a couple passes on foot, pushing through the cool evening mist, and the complex looked quiet and free of strangers lurking in the shadows.

"I'll go in. Once I have things under control, I'll signal you from the window," I told Aaron.

"I'm coming with you."

I'd thought it through, and I figured that keeping the two brothers apart would be the best thing. I didn't mind violence, but I didn't want to be in the middle of two brothers killing each other. With the well-used pistol in my pocket, courtesy of Aaron's impressive collection, I was more than ready to face Tanner alone.

"I think you should stay here. Things could get ugly."

"You think he'll fight back."

"Wouldn't you?"

"Sure."

"So stay here. I'll take care of it."

I didn't wait for his reply, already stepping off the curb. But it came as to no surprise when I felt Aaron's presence behind me. It was a free country, and he was a big boy. Not my place to order him to stay.

Silent as the heavy night, we made our way into the apartment complex, courtesy of a kid taking a smoke break at the gate. He nodded to us, eyes glazed. I could smell the beer on him and knew he wouldn't remember our brief exchange in the morning.

Deeper into the rehabbed set of buildings we went, music thumping at regular intervals. I'd forgotten it was Friday, but the inhabitants of the complex hadn't. We passed more party-goers, all holding drinks. They barely paid us any attention. We were just two more guys coming to party.

Lucky for us, Tanner's hallway was empty. There was no music coming from inside, and the telltale strip of light under the door was absent. Aaron and I exchanged a look, and I went at the lock with my kit as Aaron stood watch. I tried to be as quiet as I could but was thankful for the revelry throughout the complex because to my highly-tuned hearing the lock pick sounded like clanging pots and pans.

With a final click, I turned the handle, pushing slowly in case Tanner had the chain lock set. It wasn't, and we swept into the room, weapons and eyes scanning the area. The blinds were all drawn and it took a few long seconds for my eyes to adjust to the darkness. When they did, my finger tightened on the trigger.

Tanner was sitting at the kitchen table, staring at us. There were two pistols in front of him, along with what could have been cleaning gear. I smelled the familiar odor of CLP (Cleaner, Lubricant, Preservative), a lifelong memory from the Marine Corps and countless hours spent making weapons spotless.

None of us moved. I wasn't about to shoot an unarmed man, even if he did have pistols sitting inches from his hand. It was an easy shot, and he would have a chance.

"You found me," Tanner said, his tone of voice matter-of-fact, revealing nothing.

"What were you doing at the park, Tanner?" Aaron asked. I sensed a hint of desperation in his voice, like he really wanted his brother to be the good guy. Too bad things were stacked on the dark side.

Tanner cocked his head, and in the low light, I thought I saw him give an amused smile.

"I thought that would've been obvious," he said. "Ulysses was going to kill you, and I wasn't going to let that happen."

"You killed him?" Aaron asked, incredulous.

"Of course."

"How did you know—?"

"—that he was going to kill you? Did you really think you were the only mole I had in there? Your boss put two and two together and someone fingered you for the video."

Silence except for the muted bass thumping down the hall.

"So what now?" Aaron asked. He hadn't dropped his weapon's sights, and the two of us stood side by side, crosshairs locked on Tanner. Aaron believed Tanner about as much as I did. It was too convenient. He could've killed Ulysses just to further his own plans. Sure it was nice that he'd presumably saved his brother's life, but it was really Tanner's word against a dead man's.

"I think you should leave town," Tanner said. "I've got things to finish, and then I'll come find you."

He really thought we were just going to let him walk away. I was about to tell him to go to hell. Aaron spoke first.

"I'm with NCIS, goddammit! I can't let you go, Tanner. You're a fucking criminal!"

You could feel the years of frustration bursting forth with the revelation. I was surprised, but not as surprised as Tanner. His eyes went wide, and if there'd been light in the room, I was sure we would've seen his face become ashen.

"Say something!" Aaron yelled, moving closer to his brother, pistol aimed at Tanner's head.

Tanner raised his hands to shoulder level. His mouth kept opening and closing like a fish taking its dying breaths on some sandy beach.

Aaron rushed forward and grabbed his brother by the front of the shirt, jerking him roughly from the chair and tossing him to the floor. I shifted with their movement to keep my aim squarely on Tanner.

"You took away my career! If you hadn't been such a fuck up, I might still be with my friends right now. Can't you see what you've done, what you've screwed up? It's not all about you, Tanner. Fuck!" He kicked his brother in the ribs, eliciting a pained grunt from Tanner. Despite the assault, Tanner didn't fight back.

He was trying to say something, but the kick had blasted the air from his lungs. Aaron bent down and I tensed. The former Raider was losing it now, forgetting the proximity voided much of the pistol's effectiveness.

This time Tanner blocked the kick with his hands and held Aaron's foot until the younger brother wrenched it free. Tanner held up a hand, asking for a second to catch his breath. Aaron gave it to him and I took a step closer, still well out of arm's reach.

"I didn't know," Tanner said finally. He was gulping in air now.

"You weren't supposed to know, you idiot," Aaron said. "It's called being undercover, only I had to go undercover to put my brother in jail."

Aaron's breathing almost matched Tanner's now. He was choking up with emotion as he glared at his brother.

A single tear ran down Tanner's face.

"You were never supposed to be part of this," Tanner said, shaking his head sadly. He looked over at me, but if he was looking for help, he was asking the wrong guy. His eyes settled on Aaron again. "You don't understand."

Aaron raised his pistol hand this time, like he was going to slam the butt of the weapon down on Tanner's face. "What don't I understand, Tanner, is why you're a piece-of-shit drug dealer that never gave two shits about anyone but himself."

"I'm sorry you feel that way." His voice sagged, and he sat up slowly, hand still raised to ward off another blow. "There are things I couldn't tell you. I had to keep you safe. But it looks like those assholes took care of that." His eyes hardened now, not at Aaron, but at some unseen foe off in the distance. "I should have told you."

"Told me what?"

Tanner looked up at his brother, his eyes softening now. "They came to me in Lejeune. They said I could make a difference. They said I could make things right."

"What are you talking about?" Aaron growled impatiently. His weapon was aimed at Tanner's head again.

"I work for them too, Aaron. I work for NCIS."

CHAPTER TWENTY-FOUR

Tanner's blunt admission echoed in my head as I watched Aaron take first one step back, then another.

"I don't believe you," Aaron said.

"It's true, I promise," Tanner said. "They came to me when the Jacksonville cops arrested me. That's when they gave me the ultimatum, help them or stay in jail. After that I was on a pretty short leash, but I proved myself. Things got heavy quick. They even helped me bring weapons and drugs into the country so we could build dossiers on the suppliers."

"Bullshit."

"They'll be here soon. Ask them."

"Who?"

"My NCIS handlers."

Aaron glanced at me. He was thinking the same thing I was. It couldn't be a coincidence. We'd called in NCIS and were supposed to be meeting them later that night. Was it true that they were coming to see Tanner first? Were they even the same guys?

"What time?" I asked.

Tanner looked at his watch. "Ten minutes."

"Then we wait," Aaron declared, pointing to the chair that Tanner had recently vacated. "You try anything..."

The threat lingered in the air like a hawk gliding over a wheat field. Tanner took a seat at the kitchen table and I gathered the loaded pistols and stuffed them into my pockets. The only thing left to do was wait. I flipped on the lights and leaned against the wall.

THE KNOCK CAME EXACTLY ten minutes later. Aaron went to the door and looked through the peep hole. He looked back at me and nodded. It must be the same guys.

Aaron opened the door, his pistol held behind his back. Four men strode in wearing a variety of casual civilian attire. The first guy was the shortest, burly going on fat. He came straight in, but the other three, each a head taller than the first guy, fanned out and waited.

"It's good to see the Gray brothers together again," the man said in a gravelly smoker's voice that ended with a chuckle.

No one else in the room was amused. Tanner and Aaron were both staring at the man with open contempt.

"Oh, come on, guys, I thought you'd like this little twist," the man continued, even going so far as to pat Aaron on the shoulder, an action that elicited an immediate flinch from the younger Gray.

"Why didn't you tell us?" Tanner asked.

"I was going to tell you at some point." Then his gaze shifted and rested on me. "And this must be the famous Daniel Briggs. I've gotta say, Briggs, you were the surprise of this whole op."

I didn't like the man's attitude.

"Who is this guy?" I asked Aaron.

"Caden Spade," the NCIS agent answered with a low bow.

"Now, if you wouldn't mind, I'd like to have a word with the Grays." He was all smiles.

"I think I'll stay," I said.

Spade looked to Tanner and then to Aaron. Both men nodded.

"Fine," Spade said, but his demeanor had soured perceptibly. The guy radiated sleaze. I wondered if Aaron or Tanner felt the same. How did a guy like that become an NCIS agent? All the NCIS guys I'd met were sharp and professional. This guy smelled more like a beat cop who'd been on the take since getting his badge. "It's time to close up shop, boys. Headquarters wants you to pack your things and head East for a thorough debriefing. Leave everything you have with me, and we'll close out the operation."

"You're kidding," Tanner said. "We've almost got it buttoned up."

"Do you know who's behind it?" Spade asked.

Tanner hesitated. "No, but I'm close. We've got two or three suspects; Howard Bishop is on the hook—"

"You've had enough time, Tanner," Spade said with more than a touch of condescension. "You did good, though. Let us big boys take it from here."

"I didn't throw away my career to put up with this bullshit," Aaron said, taking a menacing step toward Agent Spade.

"It's not your call," Spade said, unconcerned by the unanimous Gray vote.

"Whose call is it?" Aaron asked, his pistol now at his side. I saw two of the oversized security guards lock eyes on the weapon.

"It's my call. Now, for the last time, give me what you've got and pack up your shit." Spade was already moving to the door, a cell phone appearing in his meaty hand.

"Fuck you," Aaron spat.

All three gorillas looked to their boss. Spade turned slowly and said, "Don't forget, I know where you live," he said, pointing at Aaron, and then he shifted to Tanner, "and we still have access to your safety deposit boxes, so really I already have everything we need. Look, guys, we can do this the easy way or the hard way. Either you play along or I put you in the clink right now. Your call."

The Gray brothers exchanged glances as I kept watching Spade, who was putting the cell phone to his ear. The funny thing was that I never saw him press any of the buttons. Then it all came together, and I saw Spade give the tiniest nod to his three men. Tanner and Aaron didn't see it, but I did. Even as I opened my mouth to roar a warning, three long black pistols, their barrels extended by silencers, slipped out of hidden holsters.

The room and its occupants slowed as my senses snapped into the next dimension. I lunged left, pistol firing, and saw Aaron doing the same. The kitchen table flipped away from Tanner, but not before I saw a spout of crimson blood spew from his neck.

Silenced rounds were drowned out by the booming from mine and Aaron's pistols. We focused on the armed men, and I was shocked to see the heavyset Spade already bursting through the door, shielding himself with the bodies of his men. Two had already fallen. The third took two of my bullets through the chest and another three from Aaron.

By the time we'd dealt with the immediate threat, Spade was gone, a trail of blood running out the door.

"Shit," Aaron was saying. I glanced back and saw him kneeling next to his brother. He had a dish cloth pressed to Tanner's neck.

I stuck my head into the hallway, and when no rounds greeted me, I looked out farther. Spade had taken the stairs and I was halfway out the door in pursuit when Aaron called to me. "We need to take him to the hospital."

I considered ignoring him. I could catch up to Spade if I left now. But when I looked back for the last time, I saw the pleading in Aaron's eyes and the way his brother's body hung slack in his arms. I ran back into the room and felt for a pulse. It was faint but there.

Blood was coming out in warm gushes between Aaron's fingers, and the dish towel was already soaked through. Tanner's face was slack and pallid. I checked his pulse again. Nothing.

Without thinking, I started compressions, but the blood was still pumping out of Tanner's neck as if his body was trying to mock us as we tried in vain to help.

Ever so slowly, Aaron removed his hands from his brother's neck. I kept doing compressions, and as I did, the movement dislodged the blood-soaked towel. I saw the gaping wound, like a tiger had bitten a chunk out of Tanner's neck. I'd seen plenty of bullet and shrapnel graze wounds before, but this was different.

I stopped the compressions and we just sat there for a minute.

"I'm sorry," I said.

Aaron nodded, the tears dropping down onto Tanner's corpse. With bloody hands, he picked up his pistol from the floor, and for a moment I thought I'd have to wrestle it from him. I froze as he tapped the barrel against his head, and then he bent down to kiss his brother on the forehead.

"We have to go," Aaron said, rising slowly. There were sirens now, and I could imagine the rest of the apartment complex residents hunkering down in their apartments or running away in the hopes of finding a safe haven.

We hit the hallway at a sprint, and took the stairs three at a time as we made our way to the first floor. When we burst outside, the flashing blue and red lights were close. I pointed to the trail of blood that went toward the lights. We had to go the opposite way.

"This way," I said, pointing to a fence obscured by overgrown trees.

Aaron followed without speaking, his mind probably focused on that last image of his dead brother. I couldn't think of Tanner at that moment. The thing to do was keep moving, to find a target to vent our fury on. The only name in my head, a name mentioned by Tanner just before he'd been shot, was a name I didn't recognize. Howard Bishop. We had to find Howard Bishop.

CHAPTER TWENTY-FIVE

D r. Singleton hadn't heard from Tanner Gray. It was morning and he figured the expedient thing to do was put the formula in the hands of the right man. Howard Bishop would be grateful for this even though Tanner might be annoyed at being sidestepped. What did it matter? Tanner would be taken care of and he, Dr. Lionel Singleton, would be given a laboratory without limits. It was like getting to take over Santa's workshop; it made Singleton giddy just thinking about it.

Of course, there was always the money to consider, but money had always been a mere passing thought. When you came from money, you just thought of it differently, at least that was how he'd been raised. Money was a tool and not the end all. Money bought houses and toys.

Singleton had a house he loved and all the toys he needed. What he really wanted was to pursue his lifelong dream of making his own name in the medical community. His father had been a surgeon, and his grandfather held numerous patents, but Lionel had always been drawn to drugs. He never dabbled with them personally, other than the one prescription for a pain killer he'd taken at age seventeen after having his wisdom teeth extracted.

But every developed country in the world depended on drugs and vaccines to keep their populace safe. Singleton knew the truth and understood that most of his future developments would build off the work of others. Like an artist who felt that no art was truly unique, Singleton believed his gift was making the next generation of whatever it was that the world needed.

And so he'd studied Palacor's formula at length, thanks to Tanner Gray obtaining it from his unknown source. He believed he'd perfected it, indeed faster than anyone else in the field could. Singleton didn't want to be the boss. He did want to be a leader in his field, but other than managing the assistants Bishop had promised, he had no compulsion to actually lead. Leave that to men like Bishop who enjoyed getting in real and virtual fist fights. Singleton was content to spend his days in the lab and his nights on the water.

He pressed SEND, and the formula skittered off into the data sphere, its final destination the private inbox of Howard Bishop.

———

THE NEWLY REFURBISHED house was just what he'd needed. Penthouse hotel rooms were all the rage for some, but Howard Bishop preferred an architectural marvel on the coast any day. It reminded him of his place on Martha's Vineyard, and his parents' getaway in the Hamptons. All he could see was water and foggy wisps outside the window. He sighed and sipped his Bloody Mary.

A melodic ding sounded from the kitchen. Bishop looked over at his laptop. He'd long since turned off the annoying alerts from his business email account. His personal email was another matter. Established by a freelancer, recommended by an old friend, the email account was said to be impregnable. The login required a retina scan, and any other attempts to gain access would wipe out the account.

He only used the account on rare occasions, and only a handful of people had ever received the email address. He was waiting on one of those people. The man he knew as Tom had promised the formula first thing that morning. He'd already finished breakfast and had watched two hours of news before the inbox dinged.

The CEO of Bishop Pharmaceuticals rushed to the laptop and pressed his eye to the rudimentary retina scanner. A long moment later, the screen turned blue and the inbox appeared. The email wasn't from Tom, but from a Lionel Singleton. Bishop had to search his mental database for a few seconds before remembering that Singleton was the doctor who Tom had said was his go-to formula man. It was Singleton who'd perfected Palacor's drug and created something better than even that bitch, Doreen Davis, and her team could. Bishop then remembered that he'd promised this doctor a job. He'd have to see to that personally, and made a mental note to have a chat with his vice president of research.

He scanned the email and then skipped to the end when he realized it was mainly Singleton going on and on about how excited he was to have the opportunity to work with Bishop. Didn't the idiot know that no one worked *with* Bishop, but *for* him?

What did make him smile was the attachment that held the formula Tom had promised. He saved the file to his computer and then sent the formula to the head of his research department. The man was a social moron, but he could take one look at what appeared as gibberish to Bishop and tell him whether it had any potential.

His morning task finished, Bishop settled back into the

couch and returned to watching the public dismantling of
Doreen Davis and Palacor.

———

WE'D SPENT the night on the boat. Since Agent Spade knew
where Aaron lived, the island getaway was a no-go. Instead of
going there, we puttered along the coast, trying to come up
with a new game plan. With Tanner we had something, but
without him we were stuck.

A quick internet cafe search of Howard Bishop showed us
the man Tanner had mentioned. The guy was a budding
billionaire and had made his money in the pharmaceutical
world. That seemed to fit with what we'd found out so far.
Even if he wasn't *the* guy, if Tanner had him on the list, it was
likely he would lead us to whoever was behind the drug plot.

The problem was we'd never gotten the full scoop. We
knew there was a larger story, something Spade hadn't let
Aaron in on. With the weight of Tanner's death hanging over
us, we discussed the possibilities; everything from turning
ourselves in, to finding Agent Caden Spade and putting a
bullet in his head. By then we'd realized that Spade had probably gone rogue. There was no way NCIS would condone
such an operation, and they sure as hell weren't in the business of killing their own people. But without another contact
inside NCIS to help, we were stuck again. Help. We needed
help.

"I can't believe I didn't think of it," I chided myself aloud.

"What?" Aaron was doing surprisingly well considering
he'd recently watched his brother get murdered. It was a skill
Special Forces guys learned, compartmentalization, at least
until after the mission was completed.

"I've got a buddy within the FBI. Maybe he can tell us
where Bishop is."

With no other option, Aaron readily agreed, and we rushed to find somewhere to dock and find a phone.

REX HAZARD PICKED up with a bored, "Hazard."

"Hey, it's me."

"Oh, *shit*."

"I need your help."

To his credit, Rex knew when to cut the wise ass routine. "Tell me."

"Can you find out if a guy named Howard Bishop is in Seattle?"

There was a pause and then Rex said, "Bishop. Bishop. Why do I know that name?"

"I don't know. Can you find out?"

"I'll do my best. What number can I call you back at?"

I gave him the number of the payphone and hung up.

"You think he'll find Bishop?" Aaron asked.

"If anyone can, it's Rex."

IT TOOK OVER AN HOUR, but Rex got what we needed.

"I won't tell you how I got this, but Bishop just rented a place on Lake Washington, says it's in Medina. You know where that is?"

"Yeah."

He gave me the address and then asked, "How's it going out there, Snake Eyes?"

"Same old shit," I said.

Rex chuckled. "Give me a call if you need anything else. I'm sure I can scramble a couple helos if you need them."

"I wish, but thanks."

"Stay in touch, okay?"

"Sure."

I hung up and handed the address to Aaron.

"Do you know the best way to get there?"

Aaron thought for a second and then said, "Yeah, and I think we can take the boat."

IT WAS ONLY a few miles to where Bishop was staying, but because we went by boat we had to go through the locks in Ballard. We got stuck behind a few fishing boats, but once we skirted around them it was pretty easy going except for occasionally dodging the wayward weekend sailors.

Even though a lot of coastline was covered in trees, we could still make out the heavy outlines of multi-million dollar mansions overlooking the water. We played fishermen, working our way south on the eastern edge of Lake Washington. When we passed the place Bishop was supposedly staying, I kept my eyes on my fishing line, even getting a hit from some unseen fish who thought better of the rubber snack.

By the time we got a few houses away, I had a good idea of how we should approach. Coming in from the road was risky. A place like that was sure to have a gate or some type of barrier to its entry, so the best way to come in was from the water. I decided to do what I'd done in the past and pull out my old acting repertoire.

————

HOWARD BISHOP HAD JUST WOKEN from his nap when the sound of a sputtering motor caught his attention. He'd fallen asleep in the U-shaped sectional overlooking Lake Washington, and he now looked toward the water with interest. A boat was just coming into view, and he saw two men bent over a motor that seemed to be the cause of the sputtering.

One of the men kept throwing his arms up in the air in

apparent consternation. The other guy took turns fiddling with the motor and turning to give his companion a piece of his mind.

Bishop laughed. It reminded him of the surly fishermen he used to watch in the Northeast who were just coming back in from their early morning voyages. Some would inevitably be drunk, yelling obscenities at their boat mates. The duo on the water looked like a two-man reenactment of the same.

He wandered out to the second-level patio and finally he heard the men's voices, coarse and annoyed. Neither looked up from their source of distress until they'd almost hit the dock at the end of Bishop's rental property. One noticed first, a blonde fellow with a beard, and was quick enough to jump out of the boat, onto the wooden dock, thus slowing the boat's trajectory. Together, the two men wrestled the vessel in, continuing their argument all the while.

"Can I call someone for you?" Bishop yelled down.

Both men looked up in surprise. After a few seconds of quiet deliberation, the blonde man yelled back.

"Do you mind if we use your phone? My uncle's just up the way, and he can come pick us up."

Bishop was in a charitable mood attributed to one of many factors, possibly the impending news from his research department, the billions he was soon to acquire, or the two Bloody Marys and three screwdrivers he'd had.

"Sure, come on up."

The blonde man waved his thanks and said he'd be up in a minute.

When the young man arrived at the foot of the stairs leading up to the lower level, Bishop noticed he was scruffier than he'd first thought. He looked like the fishermen of his youth, with a white smile to go along with the growing beard.

"The phone's upstairs," Bishop said, pointing up toward the house.

"I really appreciate this, Sir. My brother forgot his cell phone again. Next time he's swimming home."

Bishop laughed along with the blonde stranger and waved him upstairs.

When they got to the living room, Bishop showed the man where the home phone was as he shuffled into the kitchen to see if he'd gotten a reply. He had. A blue light was blinking on his screen. It was from his research director; the little red flag indicated urgent.

Butterflies fluttered in Bishop's stomach as he opened his email folder and read the first line.

Formula looks to be incomplete. Confirmed authenticity of Palacor compound, but the rest is lacking. Will know more soon.

BISHOP READ the concise message again and then a third time. Then he opened the attachment that Singleton had sent. He had no idea what he was looking at, but he wondered if he'd somehow emailed it incorrectly. He had no way of knowing but sent it to his research director a second time, just in case.

When he looked up, he was surprised to see the blonde man standing next to him. He hadn't heard any of the phone conversation. Maybe it was just that he'd been so absorbed in the message...

"We need to talk, Mr. Bishop," the man said, the winning smile gone. He looked cold and menacing now, like a viper, steady and zeroed in.

Bishop staggered back, suddenly aware of the confines of the room. He hadn't seen any need for added security. He rarely traveled with bodyguards unless he was attending a public event or traveling overseas. But still he was no shrinking violet. He'd been a boxer in his youth, and he still worked the bag three times a week to keep off the extra pounds.

"Who are you?" Bishop demanded. That was when the second man stepped into the room. This one's face looked even harder, yet somehow familiar.

"Do you know a man named Tanner Gray?" the blonde one asked.

"Tanner who? No. I don't know a Tanner Gray," Bishop managed to get out without stammering. There was something about the two men that promised pain should his answer be wrong. "Now, I asked you a question. Who are you, and what do you want?"

"What about Dr. Singleton? Do you know him?" the same man asked.

He tried to keep the surprise from his face, but he must have failed because he saw recognition in the blonde man's eyes.

"I don't *know* him, but I know *of* him," Bishop said. Not quite a lie. He'd never met Singleton.

"How do you know *of* Dr. Singleton?"

The second man was moving closer now. Bishop could smell the sweat and motor oil on the man.

"I'm sorry, gentlemen, but I'm expecting a guest soon. If you could please leave before I call the police." He tried to use his most CEO-like voice, the one he used on new hires and new fires. It didn't work. The men just stared at him with undisguised menace.

The man with the dark hair pulled a pistol out from under his shirt and pointed it at Bishop.

"I'm not in a very good mood right now, Mr. Bishop, so I suggest you answer my friend's questions, or the maid will be cleaning your brains off the kitchen floor."

There was so much anger in the man's eyes that Bishop's legs started shaking. Then, because he had the talent for reading people, even in times of extreme duress, he saw the sadness lining the man's features. *He's lost someone*, Bishop thought to himself. Nothing else could push a man to such extremes. That revelation made Bishop back away until he bumped up against the oversized marble island.

Bishop was a vain man, but not a stupid one. He knew when he was outnumbered, and he valued his life above all else. And so, it was with the number one goal of self-preservation that Bishop asked, "What do you want to know?"

CHAPTER TWENTY-SIX

Senator Lasky thanked her driver, requesting he return in an hour. Howard Bishop had asked for two hours, but one hour was all Lasky was prepared to give. Alliance or not, Lasky did not consider Bishop a pleasant host; the less time spent with him the better.

She watched the car ramble out through the gate, and then the new iron barrier squealed back into place with a final thump. Turning to the front path, she admired the minimalist landscaping that included the clever use of stone and ground cover. The place gave off a Japanese vibe, and she was curious to see the house's interior, despite the man who was waiting to annoy her further.

Whether she liked it or not, Howard Bishop held the key she needed. While at first she had not believed him when he said he'd had no part in Palacor's undoing, she'd had her people do some prodding, and there were definitely things Doreen Davis was doing that she had not been candid about.

Senator Lasky did not believe in coincidences, so she walked down the brick path to the massive front door with a fair amount of caution. Bishop was not one to be trifled with, but then again, neither was she.

————

BY THE TIME the senator arrived, I'd pretty much guessed that when Bishop referred to "Tom," he was indeed referencing Tanner. The pharma CEO described him to a T, and I could feel the tension radiating off of Aaron.

Bishop told us about his meeting with Tanner. He recounted how Tanner had sold him on a modified version of Palacor's drug compound. Bishop was told it was the next big thing, and that it would be worth billions, maybe even trillions. Tanner had told him about the pending news, the video of the "juice rooms."

So you can imagine our surprise when he announced that his guest was none other than Senator Janet Lasky, the Washington State representative who'd lost one son to war and the other to PTSD. When asked why Lasky was part of Bishop's plan, his answer was simply, "Lasky can get it approved."

He explained how Palacor had already been through much of the FDA's approval process, and with the ever-increasing need for a drug to combat the effects of PTSD, and a near-presidential mandate to head off the rising suicide rates of veterans, a modified version of the same drug would be easy to fast-track, with Lasky's help, of course.

It sounded to me like Lasky had made a deal with the devil. Would I have done the same? I didn't know. Was it smart to sacrifice a handful of men to save thousands?

Bishop promised to play nice, and we promised to stay out of the way. It was Aaron's idea to let things roll. I think he wanted to see if Lasky was a willing partner, or just another political patsy Bishop had wrangled.

BISHOP'S WHEELS WERE TURNING. With two armed men in the house, he walked as steadily as he could to the front door. After taking a deep breath to steady his frazzled nerves, he plastered on his best glad-handing smile and opened the door.

"Senator, thank you so much for coming to see me."

Senator Lasky looked more annoyed than usual, and Bishop wondered how she would feel if she knew that men with guns were watching from the next room. If he was lucky, and that was a very big IF, given the demeanor of the two men, especially the one with the brown hair, he might end this meeting with a deal in hand. After all, he had done nothing wrong, and to the ever astute Bishop, the strangers felt more like vigilante good-guys than hired assassins.

Lasky was saying something about the architecture of the home, but he barely heard her. He answered with a hurried, "I'm not sure who built it, but I'd be happy to find out."

Of all the times to catch Lasky at a chatty moment, this was the worst.

"Would you like a drink?" he asked.

She gave him a disapproving look like it was too early for cocktails, and then she said, "I'll have a glass of wine, if you have it."

He was happy to oblige, and managed to down a shot of bourbon as he fetched the platter of prepared appetizers from the fridge. If he was going to last the day with a gun aimed at the back of his head, he was going to need more than a little liquid fortification.

———

WE WATCHED and listened from the laundry room. We'd taken a risk letting Bishop meet with the senator, but he appeared to be behaving, and we desperately needed more information. By Bishop's own admission, and I was leaning toward believing him, he'd just been the right guy in the right place at the right time. He was probably correct, and I imagined Tanner had chosen Bishop because of his "win at any cost" attitude.

The guy smelled like a snake oil salesman, and yet he didn't necessarily give off the vibe that he was willing to risk his entire company to do something so overtly illegal as to kill people.

As for the senator, I only knew about her because of her sons. When she ran for office, I'd still been part of the real world, and a lot of us cheered when the mother of two dead soldiers snatched victory like a lone knight slashing through a horde of the enemy.

Her body language told me that she had little, if any, respect for Bishop. Did they have a history together, or was she just more in tune with his general character as I was? I settled in to see. It would turn out to be a very interesting conversation.

———

"WE'RE GOING to do this out of the public eye for the time being," Senator Lasky was explaining. "Despite what's happening with Palacor, the president himself promised me that he will put his full weight behind the fast track. He wants the solution almost as much as I do."

Bishop grinned, despite the knowledge that two men were watching and waiting, guns probably pointed at the back of his head.

"And you're sure you can get it through?" he asked.

"As long as the trials go as planned, my contacts at the FDA tell me it shouldn't be a problem."

Bishop was about to ask her about the patent process, and how his company would wade through that swamp, when his laptop dinged. He froze, remembering that the last time he'd been at the computer was when his research director told him the news about Singleton's formula. FORMULA INCOMPLETE, were the words that came back to him.

"Do you mind if I get that?" he asked, pointing to the laptop on the kitchen counter.

Lasky gave him a look, but nodded.

He was careful not to make any sudden moves. He didn't want the armed visitors to think he was calling for help. Bishop didn't doubt they would shoot him, and he had no desire to die that day. Deliberately turning the laptop screen toward the laundry room door, he stood at an angle so that the men could see that he was just checking his email. The short message made his heart sink.

The same formula as before. What am I missing?

Howard Bishop weighed his options. He could make a run for it. At best he could get to the street, and maybe a cop would be driving by and help him. Bishop dismissed that option as quickly as it had come to him.

After reading the message again, and giving a reassuring nod to the cracked laundry room door, Bishop decided that the best course of action was to tell the truth. He was about to call the strangers out when he heard a familiar sound. He looked toward the front door and realized it was the metal gate at the top of the drive. The last thing he needed was more surprise guests.

When the men in the laundry room didn't make a move, Bishop went to the video monitor and clicked it on. Two dark sedans were pulling into the drive.

Senator Lasky got up.

"Who's that?" she asked.

"I wasn't expecting—"

His next words were cut off by a loud crack and then another. The front door exploded inward and dark figures streamed in.

———

I COUNTED five men with assault rifles, and then a sixth moving swiftly into the house. The last man had his arm in a sling, and Aaron hissed, "Caden Spade."

For a second I thought he'd somehow followed us, but he made his way straight toward Howard Bishop.

"What is the meaning of this?" Bishop asked.

"Someone wants to talk to you," Spade said. He grinned at Lasky and said, "Good to see you, Senator."

Another man walked in through the busted front door. He was short, probably under five feet. While he had a thin frame, his potbelly protruded awkwardly from his torso.

I looked at Aaron, but he shook his head, telling me he didn't know who the guy was either.

If the living room wasn't filled with guys with guns, I might've been amused. We would have a temporary advantage if we came out blazing. Everyone's attention was focused on the newest stranger and Bishop. As I listened to the tête-à-tête, I started marking my targets. If things went to hell, I'd be ready, and The Beast would be too.

———

"HELLO, HOWARD," said Stanley Rosenbaum, the founder and CEO of SRT Pharmaceuticals.

Bishop's eyes narrowed. "What are you doing here?"

"Oh, you know how I love to make a dramatic entrance.

Was that dramatic enough for you?" Rosenbaum smirked and turned his attention to Senator Lasky. "And may I say what a pleasure it is seeing you again, Senator." Lasky tried to look indignant, but she looked more like she'd just sucked on a sour lemon. "I really wish you'd come to me instead of accepting Howard's invitation."

Lasky found her voice. "If you gentlemen have business to discuss, I am happy to leave you to it."

Rosenbaum shook his head. "You're not going anywhere, Senator. I'm afraid you'll have to live with the consequences of your actions. But please do have a seat."

The Senator's fists were clenched, and she looked like she was going to say something. She took a seat instead, doing her best to keep the tears at bay.

"As for you," Rosenbaum said, directing his words back at Bishop. "Have you had fun on your little adventure?"

Bishop glared at his former friend. The two had been inseparable in their twenties. They spent hours over coffee and ramen noodles plotting their futures of taking over the world. Rosenbaum hadn't grown up wealthy, but he had connections to investment seed money. The plan had always been to come up with a concept that would change the world, and make them both filthy rich in the process.

Almost overnight, everything had changed. Rosenbaum met Bishop at the library they often used for marathon brainstorming sessions, and told him that he was taking his idea and starting his own company. He'd said that the investors wanted a single founder, not two, and that he was prepared to compensate Bishop for his time. He slid a check for ten thousand dollars across the table along with a non-compete agreement.

Bishop was floored. It had been his idea to jump into the pharmaceutical world, and he'd done the majority of the research for their business plan and initial startup. The plan was for him to be the CEO and Rosenbaum the COO. Bishop pleaded with his friend to reconsider, but Rosenbaum would not budge.

He'd ripped up the check and the non-compete, and just like that, they'd become competitors. That had been over thirty years ago, and still the sting of that meeting hurt Bishop. It had helped mold him into the ruthless businessman he'd become.

Now, with Rosenbaum standing in front of him with that same know-it-all smirk, Bishop had the sinking feeling that he'd once again underestimated his enemy.

"So, was it fun or not?" Rosenbaum teased.

"Was *what* fun?"

"Your little intrigue, the maze I sent you scurrying into." When Bishop didn't reply, Rosenbaum laughed and said, "You've always been easy to control, Howard."

The sinking feeling blossomed into panic, and Bishop's chest tightened. He felt like he was going to pass out.

"Cat got your tongue?" Rosenbaum asked, chomping his teeth through his grin. "That's not like you, Howard. I expected more, maybe a few of your famous curses?"

Bishop wished he could bash the man's face in. The world thought Rosenbaum was a saint, but he knew better. Rosenbaum was a thief, even though he'd never been able to prove it. Rosenbaum's company always seemed to be one step ahead. Now Rosenbaum confirmed Bishop's worst fears.

"It was all me, old buddy, old pal. I was the one pulling the strings. Do you know how many moles I have in Bishop Pharmaceuticals? And it was so easy. Everyone hates you, Howard, even your own people!"

So, it was happening again. He'd been outmaneuvered by the little shit. There was no coming back from this. Bishop knew in his soul that Rosenbaum was here because it was all over. That fact was confirmed a moment later when Rosenbaum said, "With friends in the VA like Dr. Singleton, and Mr. Spade here, who's been working from inside NCIS, we've done the impossible. Your company will be dismantled, and I'll get the scraps for pennies on the dollar. With you gone, in addition to Doreen and Palacor on the way out as well, I'll be the last player left. With one grand stroke I've wiped out numbers one and three, leaving me right where I should be – on top."

Something about the blunt admission calmed Bishop. He didn't know why, but it felt like a weight had been lifted. He'd spent his entire adult life chasing after Rosenbaum, and the sneaky bastard always seemed to sniff out his next move. Now that he knew the truth, that the entire game had been rigged, a measure of finality and peace entered Bishop's psyche. He didn't live with regrets. He was a fighter, and he'd bobbed and weaved to the best of his abilities. If that wasn't good enough, at least he'd given it his all.

Bishop smiled. "At least I have my life."

Rosenbaum clicked his tongue, then said, "About that..." He pointed to the man standing to his left, and the last thing Howard Bishop saw was the man pulling the trigger.

CHAPTER TWENTY-SEVEN

Senator Lasky screamed as Howard Bishop's body hit the floor, the back of his head now splattered on the tile backsplash.

"I'm sorry you had to see that, Senator," Rosenbaum said. "You can't say he didn't have it coming."

"What is wrong with you?" Lasky was now in tears, her entire body shaking uncontrollably.

Rosenbaum looked around comically. "Who, me?" He laughed at himself like a child telling a knock-knock joke.

"You're a monster," Lasky said, sliding further down the couch.

Rosenbaum shrugged. "You have to admit that I'm pretty good at it, though. Surely, you see the brilliance behind it. I mean, who else could have done what I did?"

"And the drug? Was that all a lie too?"

Rosenbaum ignored the question and said, "Can't you see that the system is broken, Senator? Money can buy anything. Hell, I bought you, and you didn't even know it. How sad is that?"

"You didn't buy me," Lasky said.

"Yes, I did. You did exactly what I wanted. You let Doreen Davis sink and switched your allegiance to Howard there just so you could get what you wanted."

"That's not what happened."

"Isn't it? Howard got his hands on a supposed super drug that would alleviate the symptoms of PTSD. He called you and you took the bait because Palacor is under investigation. Where do you think that came from? Me. I'm the one who planted everything, from the lost Palacor shipments purchased in Taiwan and provided to a local drug dealer, to the bogus NCIS operation involving the two Gray kids that was supposed to be a manhunt for whoever was behind my made-up government manipulation. The only problem was the manhunt should have been for me." Rosenbaum grinned. Lasky shrank back from the maniacal gleam in the man's eyes. "And so here we are. I've pulled the strings and accomplished my coup. It's just too bad you won't be around to see it come to full fruition." He turned and spoke to the man in the arm sling. "Make it look like a lover's quarrel; I think the media will like that."

Rosenbaum headed for the door as two of his men slung their weapons and converged on Senator Lasky. There was nowhere to run. Lasky was about to scream when a crashing sound came from the kitchen, followed by gunshots. Two men emerged from a room just off the kitchen and waded into the skirmish, firing calmly.

Lasky saw two of Rosenbaum's men go down without getting off a shot. Without thinking, she dropped to the floor and covered her head with her hands.

———

NCIS Agent Caden Spade spun around just as a bullet hit him in his wounded arm. He took the shot with a grunt as he raised his good hand to return fire with his pistol. When he looked over his sights, his eyes bulged. Aaron Gray was firing and running for the front door, and the Briggs guy was staring straight at Spade.

There was something wrong with his face. It didn't look human. It had the appearance of an animal mask or something. But the eyes were the worst. Spade felt them boring into him like a steel ice pick.

Spade fired at Briggs but somehow all of his shots went wide. Time slowed to a crawl. Briggs kept shooting, and Spade sensed that the sniper was taking his men out one by one even as rounds cracked into the wall behind him. Suddenly, Spade realized he was the only one firing.

When his pistol clicked empty, Spade tried to eject the magazine, but there was a sudden stinging pain, and then a shooting fire ran up his arm. He looked down at where his weapon had been and found that the pistol and three of his fingers were no longer there.

Blood poured from his hand as the specter that was Briggs descended upon him. Spade's world went black.

———

ROSENBAUM'S INABILITY TO feel emotion helped him now. He didn't panic; he just ran. He got all the way to the first car, even opened the driver's side door before he sensed a pursuer right behind him. Rosenbaum turned and got slammed into the side of the car. A red-faced young man was holding a gun to his head.

"Where do you think you're going?" the man asked.

Rosenbaum cocked his head.

"You're Aaron Gray."

"And you're a piece of shit," Gray said.

There were a thousand things Rosenbaum could have said. This was one of the benefits of being emotionally bereft. He had the ability to detach completely from the outside world. As a child, he remembered watching himself be bullied, like an out-of-body experience, feeling the physical pain, but never experiencing sadness or fear. His mother had called him a little freak, and he supposed she had been correct.

But over the years he'd learned to fake emotion. He'd smile and laugh with classmates to fit in. When a situation warranted sadness, he pulled out the sad face he'd practiced in front of the bathroom mirror.

It was in business where his hidden talent really set him apart from others. He could fire an entire division without feeling an ounce of regret.

And now he stared at Aaron Gray with open curiosity. What was there to say, really?

Rosenbaum's face was blank and devoid of humanity when he asked, "Do you miss your dead brother?"

———

SENATOR LASKY LOOKED up from her prone position and flinched as a single shot sounded from somewhere outside. She could smell the death in the room and chanced a glance up. There was one man standing and looking toward the door. When he sensed her movement, he shifted his attention to her.

"Are you okay?" he asked.

Lasky nodded and then winced when another form came through the front door. It was the second man she'd seen bursting from what she now realized was the laundry room. The young man was dragging something, a body.

"Is he dead?" the blonde man asked.

"No," the other replied. "Is *he?*" the second man asked, pointing to a form at the other man's feet.

"No."

The two men stared at each other. Lasky could see their chests rising and falling, slow and steady. She wondered if that was what her sons had felt after a firefight, when the adrenaline of near death began to wane. The thought brought fresh tears to her eyes, and she collapsed to her knees and mourned again for her children.

———

IT WAS A STRANGE FEELING. It was not the fact that we'd just killed a room full of bad guys, but that I hadn't let go of myself. The Beast had been there the entire time, helping me focus and do what needed to be done, but he never took over. The proof was lying at my feet, where Agent Spade lay bleeding from his hand, but still very much alive.

Senator Lasky was sobbing in the living room, and Aaron looked like he was about to do the same. His eyes were bloodshot red, but he held my gaze with the intensity of a warrior who'd just tempted fate and came out unscathed. Relatively unscathed.

"What was that shot?" I asked. I didn't know if Aaron had taken Rosenbaum down with the pistol.

"I figured we should get someone's attention."

I was going to ask what he meant, but on cue, the screaming wails of police sirens invaded our brief quiet.

"What's the plan?"

Aaron looked over at Senator Lasky, who'd managed to stand up and was taking tentative steps our way.

"Maybe we should ask the senator," he said.

Lasky's smeared mascara made her look like a weeping

raccoon, but she'd regained a bit of her composure and said, "I'll take care of it."

THE COPS SWARMED in a minute later, guns at the ready, yelling commands even though the three of us had our hands in the air.

"*Holy shit!*" one of the cops exclaimed.

Another cop took one look around before puking on the guy standing next to him.

An older police officer charged in. He looked salty as hell with his gray hair and wrinkles. He reminded me of a crusty sergeant major I'd once served with. His eyes flicked from us to the bodies and back again. Then he must have recognized Senator Lasky because he asked her, "You wanna tell me what the hell happened here, Ma'am?"

She pointed at Aaron and me. "These men saved my life, Officer."

"And who the hell are you?" he asked us, glaring at us like a drill sergeant.

I answered with an ironic grin. "Just a couple of dumb Marines, sir."

CHAPTER TWENTY-EIGHT

The word traveled lightning quick through the Marine pipeline. Tanner's friends, the Marine buddies from before the drug fiasco, came in droves. NCIS had spread the word, with the "polite" insistence of Senator Lasky. The truth was out about what their rogue agent had done, and the military establishment now knew the real scoop on Tanner Gray. He was no longer a pariah, but a fellow Marine to be mourned.

Senator Lasky insisted on being at the funeral and stood next to Aaron during the whole service. She didn't say it, but I knew the Gray brothers reminded her of her own sons, and it was part of her healing to be with the Gray family.

Aaron was coping as well as he could. He told me he regretted not knowing sooner the truth about his brother, that maybe it was his fault.

I had to remind him that the blame rested solely with Stanley Rosenbaum and Agent Caden Spade, both of whom were now in federal custody. As soon as the last stand in the bloody kitchen ended, Senator Lasky called the Director of the FBI and demanded a prompt investigation. Rosenbaum and Spade were now in the hands of the FBI's best, and the VA was getting a corporate version of an FBI rectal exam.

I had to hand it to Lasky. She was true to her word, and she had the rats scurrying for cover. Dr. Singleton was on the run, but the FBI was pretty confident he was hiding somewhere in Asia. It would be a year before Rosenbaum's accomplice was extradited back to the States.

The emotional conclusion came hours after the funeral, when the FBI found a cubby hidden under the toilet in Tanner's apartment. The hidden alcove contained a journal chronicling Tanner's entire duplicitous journey. It included plans, Agent Spade's instructions, and many entries where Tanner repeatedly noted his regret in taking a role in the whole affair and wondering what the consequences would be. He wasn't worried about himself, but for Aaron and the men and women being victimized.

As for me, I was coming to grips with the change inside. Luckily, after a battery of tests where I was poked and prodded by a host of stern-looking doctors, they declared that the drug from my stay in the Juice Room was completely out of my system. The IV bags the FBI confiscated were, in fact, concentrated versions of what Palacor would at some point bring to market. That, along with a steady drip of ketamine, was what kept me and the rest of the guinea pigs in a near-comatose state. One of the doctors also said that the ketamine was what had caused the strange dreams and hallucinations.

It would be a longer weaning period for the others, some of whom had been in the care of Ulysses' "treatment centers" for months as their government stipends were drained along with what was left of their lives. But the doctors said they'd be taken care of, and Senator Lasky promised to keep tabs on every single patient until they'd been released back into society. She'd even sponsored a new bill fittingly named *The Gray*

Bill, the passage of which would ensure the future care of needy veterans through advanced research and trials in areas other than standard drug related remedies. One of the first people the bill would help was Jonathan, Rose's son, who'd been found in the final Juice Room raided by Seattle Police. They were together again, and the last time I saw her, she was reading a book at his bedside, a worried look replaced by the softness of a mother caring for her long-absent son.

AND THE BEAST, he was still there. He would always be with me, padding and purring inside. But we'd come to an agreement, of sorts. In exchange for dealing with my pain, The Beast was mine to command. The Beast abhorred weakness, and in my broken state, I'd been a perfect target for takeover. No more. We were one person. I was me.

————

AARON PULLED his monster truck curbside.

"You sure I can't buy you a plane ticket?" he asked me.

"I like trains."

"What about a drink for the road? My treat?"

I smiled. Aaron didn't know that my usual routine before leaving town was to find a liquor store and snatch my good friend Jack Daniels. The bottle had been a good traveling companion, but one I didn't think I'd need anymore.

"I'm good. Thanks."

I opened the truck door and started to get out. Aaron grabbed my arm.

"Hey, if you ever need anything, call me," he said.

I turned and offered my hand. We shook on it.

"And if you're ever in Las Vegas, look me up."

"Vegas? Really?"

I grinned. "Sin City, baby. Sounds like the perfect place to start."

Aaron laughed. "You're crazy, you know that?"

"Takes one to know one."

———

WHEN THE TRAIN pulled away from the station, all I could see was the future. There was a picture there, blurry with just a vague outline, but it was there. My past was my past, and I was done looking back. For the first time in a long time, I had a future, and that simple fact gave me hope.

I had gone through the pits of hell, driving off demons and battling crippling doubts and regrets. Now the muck and mire seemed like a dream, one that I was sure I'd never see again, as long as I remembered who I was and where I was going.

Onward I went. My mission was clear and my purpose was within reach. I was saved, and now it was time to save others. I closed my eyes, offered up a prayer of thanks and drifted off to dreams of the future.

———

I hope you enjoyed this story.
If you did, please take a moment to write a review on AMAZON. Even the short ones help!

GET A FREE COPY OF THE CORPS JUSTICE PREQUEL SHORT STORY, *GOD-SPEED*, JUST FOR SUBSCRIBING AT CG-COOPER.COM

ALSO BY C. G. COOPER

The Corps Justice Series In Order:

Back To War

Council Of Patriots

Prime Asset

Presidential Shift

National Burden

Lethal Misconduct

Moral Imperative

Disavowed

Chain Of Command

Papal Justice

The Zimmer Doctrine

Sabotage

Liberty Down

Sins Of The Father

Corps Justice Short Stories:

Chosen

God-Speed

Running

The Daniel Briggs Novels:

Adrift

Fallen

Broken

Tested

The Tom Greer Novels

A Life Worth Taking

The Spy In Residence Novels

What Lies Hidden

The Alex Knight Novels:

Breakout

The Stars & Spies Series:

Backdrop

The Patriot Protocol Series:

The Patriot Protocol

The Chronicles of Benjamin Dragon:

Benjamin Dragon – Awakening

Benjamin Dragon – Legacy

Benjamin Dragon - Genesis

ABOUT THE AUTHOR

C. G. Cooper is the USA TODAY and AMAZON
BESTSELLING author of the CORPS JUSTICE novels
(including spinoffs), The Chronicles of Benjamin Dragon and
the Patriot Protocol series.

Cooper grew up in a Navy family and traveled from one
Naval base to another as he fed his love of books and a
fledgling desire to write.

Upon graduating from the University of Virginia with a
degree in Foreign Affairs, Cooper was commissioned in the

United States Marine Corps and went on to serve six years as an infantry officer. C. G. Cooper's final Marine duty station was in Nashville, Tennessee, where he fell in love with the laid-back lifestyle of Music City.

His first published novel, BACK TO WAR, came out of a need to link back to his time in the Marine Corps. That novel, written as a side project, spawned many follow-on novels, several exciting spinoffs, and catapulted Cooper's career.

Cooper lives just south of Nashville with his wife, three children, and their German shorthaired pointer, Liberty, who's become a popular character in the Corps Justice novels.

When he's not writing or hosting his podcast, Books In 30, Cooper spends time with his family, does his best to improve his golf handicap, and loves to shed light on the ongoing fight of everyday heroes.

Cooper loves hearing from readers and responds to every email personally.

To connect with C. G. Cooper visit
www.cg-cooper.com

MORE THANKS TO MY BETA READERS:

Nancy, David, Sue, Cheryl, Karen, Don, Marry, Glenda x 2, Susan, Wanda, Pam, Andrea, Carl, Carol, Kathryn, Bob, Julie, Michael, John and Marsha. You are the wind beneath my wings... or something like it.

Made in the USA
Columbia, SC
02 September 2020